The Red Star Society

The Red Star Society

This book is a work of fiction. References to real people, events, establishments, organizations, or locales are intended only to provide a sense of authenticity, and are used to advance the fictional narrative. All other characters, and all incidents and dialogue, are drawn from the author's imagination and are not to be construed as real.

The Red Star Society

Copyright © 2023 by The Laughing Man House and Cyrus Claude Spears

ISBN: 979-8-218-22412-7

www.uncrownednovel.com

Cover Design by Irina Eshpur

Book design by The Laughing Man House

Edited by Janus

Figure illustrations and title manipulations by Sirius

Royalty-Free images sourced by Pixabay

THE RED STAR SOCIETY

THE INTIMATE JOURNALS, LETTERS, AND RECOLLECTIONS OF HER MAJESTY'S ASTRONOMER: SOPESPIAN SLAINE

SIRIUS

THE LAUGHING MAN HOUSE

For Janus. For Ellis. For Irene.

For the queer found families.

ALSO BY SIRIUS

THE DRAONIR SAGA
Uncrowned
Partitioned
Condemned
*Disinherited**

Hawthorne: A Draonir Novella

THE DRAONIR SAGA: ICONOCLASTS
*Admiral Blood**

THE GENTLEMAN DEMON SERIES
Swallow You Whole

**2024*

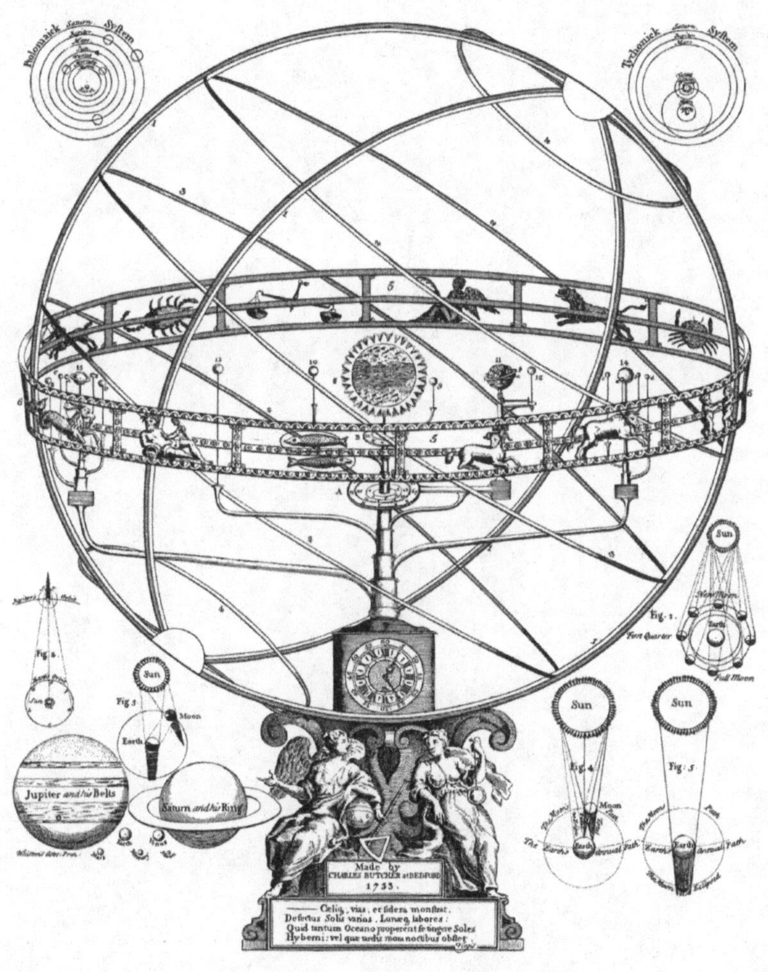

Ptolomaick Saturn System
Tychonick System
Jupiter and his Belts
Saturn and his Rings
Sun
Sun
Sun
Sun
Moon
Earth
Fig. 1
Fig. 3
Fig. 4
Fig: 5
First Quarter
Full Moon
Made by
CHARLES BUTCHER at BEDFORD
1753.
Cæliq, vias, et sidera monstrat.
Defectus Solis varios, Lunæq, labores:
Quid tantum Oceano properent se tingere Soles
Hyberni: vel quæ tardis mora noctibus obstet.

CONTENTS

Journal Entry

Introductory Notes of the Queen's Astronomer

I AM HER MAJESTY'S astronomer. To take it one step further, I believe myself to be the only royal astronomer that has ever existed within the walls of this palace. It is a position that did not need filling, a title that I am convinced they handed me for the express purpose of keeping me occupied. It suits me, so I have never complained. They gave me a telescope when I asked for one, as well as quills and ink to keep my journals. I do not want for any material means.

This is the seventh journal that I have started. All the others are finished and have been locked away in a trunk. I have a key, and Jules has the other. Anyone else will have to throw it from the tower window to get it open, in which case I believe their ad-mirable commitment to prying would circumvent any objections I might have against them doing so.

With that in mind, and in an attempt to hedge my own tendencies to ramble, I will explain the purpose of these documentations.

My name is Sopespian Slaine. I am the Court High Astronomer (Court High being the highest stratum of Her Majesty's patriciate) during the Brahntaiste Reign of East Avralaen. The year is 634, *En Kaidum.* For 300 years, we have been in *En Kaidum* under the queen who refuses to do the decent thing and die. She is pure Elvish blood, so they say—and she will reign forever—so they say. By 'they' I mean scholars who are on the queen's payroll.

Her subjects refer to her as the Eternal Summer Queen. We, the brinefolk, do not count ourselves amongst her subjects and refer to her as the Red Tide Monarch. I will return to that point.

Brinefolk or naiads, however we might be known to anyone reading this journal—are creatures of the sea. For the past five decades—a mere half-century—we have been extracted from our home in increasing numbers only to be murdered, tortured, and enslaved on land. Queen Brahntaiste is counted by her peers as a most enterprising monarch, having found a way to keep the 'pale blue devils' docile, parading us through her court with our heads bowed and our mouths shut. We are tokens of her absolute power and nothing more. We learn the language, as it is not a difficult one, yet we do not even choose our own names. So, for others, she is the Eternal Summer. For us, she is the Red Tide. Her shores are stained dark with our blood.

As of this writing, there are six of us in the palace. Yesterday, there were seven.

It was the death of Ferdinand Bauer that propelled me to form the Red Star Society. I will explain.

The Red Star Society is named for the star *Ontarous*. It is known as 'the naiad star' and it is part of the constellation *Caephaeus* (the "Great Serpent"). *Ontarous* sits at the tip of the serpent's tail, and it is brightest during the center months of the year when the weather is warm. Naiad pods have always used it to navigate as they travel from one sea to the other. With this star serving as a beacon of hope, a sign of home, and a symbol for our preservation—I gave the Society its name.

The purpose of the Red Star Society is simple. We must protect each other, for there is no one else who will come to our aid when the time comes. There is not a single human, elf, or sylph who can extend their pity far enough to put their own lives on the line for us. Furthermore, if their pity is all that propels them, we do not want it. We do not need it.

I have no way of knowing what will come next. I can only hope that we can put aside our differences to come together for the greater good. My hope is that we can transcend placing our focus on survival and turn it, instead, towards ending the reign of tyranny that has dominated our existence.

I hope that I am the last royal astronomer this palace ever sees.

Ah, and I have not yet explained Ferdinand. Poor Ferdinand, sweet Ferdinand—enchanting, capricious, and unfortunately senseless.

I will return to that point.

Sopespian

SOPESPIAN

THE RED STAR ASTRONOMER

I T WAS SOPESPIAN'S THEORY that there was a great deal in common between the ocean and the sky, which was why they were married at the horizon—content to be seen as one, joined together by a blurred seam. It was a love that sailors and pirates might begin to understand, although one they were always fated to chase.

He sought comfort in the stars, although what it gave to him was a muted kind. Through the narrow windows in his astronomy tower, the salt air stung his eyes and made his lungs burn, but it smelled like home. He would draw it through his nose and exhale slowly out of his mouth, allowing it to linger, to circulate through his blood. And doing it all while he sat at his telescope and peered at the stars through the glass-domed roof, which was enormous enough that, if he kept all the lights doused, it was almost like sitting at the bottom of the ocean and peering through the alien darkness. The stars were like jellyfish, luminescent and numerous, although the thin atmosphere of the highest tower could still not compare to the pressure of the water, and the comfort of being squeezed and held.

In the astronomy tower, staring at the sky while taking in the scent of the ocean was too much like standing beside one's father at their mother's funeral bier.

Through it all, in his adored solitude, he loved the stars. He knew every one of them by name.

Footsteps on the tower stairs shattered the gentle evening peace. Sopespian kept his grip on his telescope as he swiveled it downward to pull his eyes away from the night sky. He had doused his last lamp wick hours before, though he had no trouble seeing through the dark regardless. When the queen entered, she held a burning lamp in one hand—and had it raised just high enough to cast its burning gold aura as far as possible.

She was dressed down like a stable hand in high, worn boots and loose-fitting linens, although her collar was still fashionably high and a royal jewel glittered from its center. The only other extravagant piece was her brocade boned bodice, which laced all the way up to the back of her neck where her bright copper tresses swung as one long braid. Sopespian noticed such things only because he was putting a great deal of effort into avoiding her gaze. She might have considered it subservient, and he was content to allow her to believe so. She might not have been very flattered to know that he rarely, if ever, looked anyone in the eye.

"There are no lamps burning," she said. Her voice was clear, precise—it cut through the silence like a knife. "Are you in need of some more oil?"

"Not at all, mam," he said, fingering the knob of his telescope anxiously. "I have plenty."

"And no candles, either." She looked around. "I have seen dungeons with more gaiety."

"I can see quite well," he tried not to snip. "It is a naiad's prerogative."

"Of course." She did not keep the condescension out of her voice as she advanced a few steps into the room. "It makes sense to me, I suppose. You have to see underwater somehow, right? And some of you plunge to unimaginable depths." The way she rolled the othering word *you* around her mouth made it sound like she was going to spit. "To tell you the truth, I was not certain I would find you here. The rest of the brinefolk are in mourning."

He knew. "I find comfort in my work as its own cure for sorrow," he said.

She tilted her head. He felt as though her eyes were burning holes through his chest, yet he still did not combat them with his own. He squeezed the telescope knob between his fingers.

"Did Ferdinand mean anything to you?" she asked. She was baiting him. There would be no correct answer.

He hated her voice. He hated the way that she spoke to him. There was something about her words that made him want to cover his ears and duck his head until she stopped speaking. And yet, her word in East Avralaen was law—she could sentence him to death or grant him a commendation with the same tongue. It behooved him greatly not to ignore it.

Still, resisting the urge to hum until the noise drowned her out was enough to make sweat bead underneath his collar.

"Ferdinand…" He cleared his throat to keep his voice from breaking. "Well, of course. We all mean a great deal to one another. We are all—landed—for lack of a better term. In our—natural home we move together in communities. Here, our support of one another is more vital than ever. Even though we are all from different pods, with a few exceptions, we are family." He thought of Cahal.

Though he danced around the subject, his careful choice of words was imperative. The gods forbid that the queen be given any unpleasant reminder of her work in capturing and enslaving an entire race of creatures who were not even bound to land. Her fragile selfdom would not support accusations of tyranny. As he spoke, Sopespian studied other aspects of her face—and he found no trace of concern or guilt in the corners of her mouth or in her smooth, strong chin. Unsurprising in a woman whose lofty brow had never seen a single crease of regret.

"He pissed himself on the gibbet this morning," she said without inflection.

Sopespian bit the inside of his cheek so hard that he tasted blood.

"I know," he said. "I saw him there." He raised his eyes at last. Hers were the same soft green as sea glass, although years of piled-on contempt had hardened them.

"You came down from your tower?" She set the lamp down a stack of books, as if her hand was getting tired. "I suppose someone had to catch my librarian when he fell."

"They fainted," Sopespian said, his voice trailing off a bit at the recollection. He had already tried pushing that memory down, but he was not certain he would ever forget

Jules' face. It was already such a pale shade of grey, and it had gone nearly white when Ferdinand's head hit the gibbet planks. Jules had crumpled like a marionette with its strings cut.

"It is a pity that it was necessary," the queen said. "I dislike ruinous investments."

Sopespian's fingers twitched. He reached up to squeeze the telescope knob again and forced himself to take a deep breath.

"For what it is worth," he said, "I do not think that Ferdinand was the one who tried to poison you."

"It seems a little late for speculation," she said, "do you not agree?"

Sopespian shrugged, grinding his back teeth down on his tongue. "Did you ever ask Jules? They are your Master of Spies as well, are they not?"

She stared at him for a long moment, as if contemplating how his neck would look resting against a block. "I did not consult Jules, in fact," she said. "It was my determination that he would be unable to give me an unbiased view."

"Ah," Sopespian scoffed, "your council is otherwise known for being very objective in regards to brinefolk."

She gave him a withering look and her lips shriveled until they disappeared. "Ephraim Holst swallowed lye after the trial. He is still in the infirmary. They were close, I understand."

Sopespian closed his eyes. After everything, this was what it came down to, in the end.

"Very close," he said. "As…brothers."

It was more than that, so much more. The love that existed between Ferdinand Bauer and Ephraim Holst was unrivaled. The maestro and the singer. Gods, the stars would never forget how Ferdinand could sing.

"An innocent person does not try to poison themselves," the queen said. "He knew something."

"If he lives, *if* he lives…" Sopespian could not keep the bitterness from his words, "I hope that his wits are addled, and he cannot remember anything about what occurred. Innocence or guilt had nothing to do with it…it was an act of pure grief."

"Do you believe that?" She sounded bored. "I do not."

"Then why is he alive?" Sopespian challenged.

"I still need an orchestra in my balconies," the queen said shortly. "I do not care if his wits are addled. As long as there is music when I have need for it."

"I wonder." Sopespian could hardly swallow his rage. "I do wonder."

He knew that he was already toeing a delicate line. The queen had already lost one of her *fine acquisitions* and would not readily risk another, but her pride had limits to the verbal battering she would accept from him.

He wanted to tell her that he knew exactly why Ephraim had swallowed lye. The maestro had nothing to hide—it was that she had sentenced Ferdinand to *strivatta*. It would have been one thing for his head to be sliced off, cleanly, with an axe wielded by a compassionate hand. In this case, however, they *sawed* it off. Two executioners wielding a long, two-handed saw—better used for felling cedar trees—between them pushed it back and forth until it cut through Ferdinand's neck—bone, muscle, and all.

It was half an hour before his head fell. Before that, he screamed, and in the way that only naiads were capable. Even thinking about the terrified, agonized sound that tore from his friend's mouth was enough to make Sopespian's stomach hurt.

Ephraim would not have been able to bear the sight. Although confined to the infirmary, he undoubtedly still heard his lover's dying screams.

Sopespian could not blame him. In the end, Ephraim and Ferdinand were *hváll*—the same as Jules. They partnered for life and considered themselves espoused even in the event of one's death.

"Well." Sopespian turned his attention back to his telescope, trying to affect a bored tone. "Please forgive me, mam, I must return to my work."

"I did not come here to talk about Ephraim," she said, "I came to ask you a question."

Sopespian sucked on his teeth. "Oh?"

"I wanted to ask if you see fortunes in the stars." She glanced up at the glass ceiling. "Fortunes, or futures—do they speak to you in that way?"

Sopespian scrunched up his nose. "The stars do not talk," he said.

"There is a witch near the Red Spine who insists that they do," she responded, and sounded somewhat absent.

"I would suggest, then, sending someone out to the Red Spine to fetch her." He pushed up his sleeves with indignance. "Hester is the magician."

"Yet," she said, "not an oracle."

"I am certain one will surface," Sopespian said, "if you cast your nets deep enough, mam, who knows what you might pull up?" He wove his fingers together, sliding his hands over one another. "You do not need the stars to tell you what you already know." He meant for it to be reassuring, but he was afraid that it would come across as rude.

"I know what I am," the queen said. "I need to know what I will become." She picked up her lamp again at last, holding it high so that the light fell onto Sopespian's face. He flinched, biting down on his tongue again to resist humming.

"You are the Eternal Summer Queen," he said, "that has been so for nearly three hundred years."

"Three centuries," she said, "and yet Graueyette eludes my grasp. Dragoloth grows in power. West Avralaen bucks against my authority."

"Nations rise and fall," Sopespian said, "the stars can do nothing, save watch."

She did not seem to care for that answer. Her lip curled and she turned away, facing the stairs once again. "Why do I allow you to bury yourself in such research, if it yields nothing of use?"

He narrowed his eyes. "I do great work and it yields ample results. My experiments that you finance are the reason why Ephraim is alive."

She scoffed. "More time with your experiments, then," she said, "and less gazing at the stars."

He kept his retaliation on the tip of his tongue. She did not allow room for it, anyway. She crossed the room in a few quick steps and disappeared down the staircase.

Sopespian waited until he was certain she was gone and then he slumped on his stool, hunching his shoulders forward and burying his face in his hands. His heart pounded behind his ribs and it felt impossible to breathe, the relief of her departure overwhelmed by the anxiety that her presence left as a residual.

He waited until his hands stopped shaking—however much time passed, he was not sure. When he finally straightened up again, Sopespian slid off his stool. Abandoning his telescope for the time being, he dug through his haphazardly sorted desk until he found his fountain pen and a slip of parchment.

He had to pen a letter to Jules.

Journal Entry

Ephraim's Plight

IN MY PREVIOUS ENTRY, I mentioned the name of Ferdinand Bauer. I will return to that now, for it is necessary to know about Ephraim.

Ferdinand and Ephraim were inseparable from the start. And it is here I will make note of what might be common knowledge: East Avralaen has laws in place that severely punish the act of same-sex coupling, even amongst the non-human species. If you asked me why, I could not tell you. It was so before I ever arrived, although I understand it is not so in more civilized countries (I might interject that Dragoloth and Simisola have words, in fact, for royal consorts of the same sex as their monarch). Ferdinand and Ephraim were, in more accepted terms, *very intimate confidants*. Where one went, the other was bound to follow.

Ferdinand was a singer—a perfectly good one. Due to his nature, he had the entire court under his spell. They simply could not help themselves, they *had* to adore him. Ephraim is the Royal Music Master. A lofty title, to be sure, for someone who does more overseeing than playing (although he does play the harpsichord, and quite well).

Ephraim composed masterpieces that Ferdinand brought to life with his golden throat. Their tragedy lies, not just in how much they adored one another, but in how intertwined their lives were. They fed into each other's art as if art was wine, and they were drunk on one another.

Regarding Ferdinand, there were many rumors. He loved the human aristocracy far more than they loved him, and it is said that he fell into their drugs, their champagne, and their love far deeper than any naiad should. He strayed into the wrong arms, and he was cut down for his folly. I have mentioned it before, I believe, that he was senseless.

I will not pretend to know everything about the circumstances that led to him being accused of treason. I will say that he was tried and convicted without a shred of evidence to support the charges. Truth does not matter in the inner courts, and certainly not to the queen. I suspect that she could no longer overlook his libertine predilections and decided to make an example of him.

The day that Ferdinand was sentenced was when Ephraim decided to drink lye.

I still do not know how much he swallowed. All I know is that it was not enough to kill him. The physician said it was enough to send three human men to their graves, but poor Ephraim's nature worked against him. Instead, the lye drove him mad. He always possessed something of a passionate temper, but since that day he has become entirely unpredictable.

He mutters a great deal—talking to himself or to Ferdinand's spirit, I do not know. He seems to have periodic bouts where he forgets all that has occurred. He asks for

Ferdinand, or he talks about his latest masterpiece—yet it is always in reference to something he wrote years ago.

More than just his mind was affected by the poison. I suspect that his nerves have suffered as well. His hands tremble and he complains of pain, too much to write music or play the harpsichord. I made silver braces for his fingers, but he does not like to wear them. I tell him that they only work if they are used, but it is through one ear and out the other, so to speak. His face was not spared. He used to have two blue eyes, and now one is red. The pupil is blown and oversensitive to light. The left corner of his mouth droops, just enough to hinder his expression.

His madness drove him to shove piano wires into his ears. He could not stand to hear another voice that was not Ferdinand's. Added to his list of failures, he is not deaf, though he is harder of hearing now than he was before.

I do not know how to help him. I suspect that none of us do, although we love him, and we fear he will be the next target of the queen's wrath. Jules and I coddle him, perhaps more than is necessary, but what is to be done? Poor, inconsolable Ephraim.

Ephraim

EPHRAIM

THE INCOSOLABLE MAESTRO

LONG FINGERS TRAILED OVER ivory keys, skimming the surface without enough pressure to coax even the faintest of high, tinny notes from the harpsichord's strings. At the center of the grand ballroom, the grand instrument stole every eye. It was entirely gilt and covered in delicate, painted pink flowers with curling, soft green vines. The underside of the lid was painted with a stormy ocean scene—masterfully translucent green waves underneath a furious grey sky, each swell capped with white foam so carefully applied that it looked real enough to swipe one's fingers through. Pale blue and grey nymphs danced in the water, and towards the very edge in the upper corner—one of them rested atop a flat soaked rock, looking down on all the others.

Ephraim's hands trembled over the keys. He curled his fingers inward towards his palm to try and regain some control, unwilling to accept that nothing short of the silver braces Sopespian made—and that he refused to wear—would stop them from shaking enough for him to play. He hated the braces. They interrupted the natural, skilled movements required to coax music from the quivering brass and iron strings. The notes came out reluctant and hollow—the music did not glide through the air with graceful gaiety as it used to. Everything was mournful and heavy with the gravity of dungeon chains crashing against a marble floor.

Nothing that was beautiful. Nothing that could be sung. But then, Ephraim did not care whether he heard singing ever again. No voice could be as beautiful, no tenor as bright, and no lips as perfectly formed as his Ferdinand's—and they would never grace the halls again. Such dismal, empty chambers lacking life and luster—for all the gilded molding and brightly painted walls, for all the murals on the arched ceilings and tapestries draped beside ostentatiously tall windows—it was no longer a palace. It was a tomb. The ballroom was a sepulcher. The orchestral pit was a shrine.

When Ferdinand's head fell against the gibbet boards, the grisly sound was drowned out by cheers. Ephraim heard it all from the window of the infirmary. It was easier to remember that—the bloodthirsty, mocking dissonance wrung from a few dozen wretched throats. How their chests and lungs squeezed out such an awful crowing like fireplace bellows, feeding the raging force of the queen's ire, her vengeance. Her hatred. If Ephraim thought about that, he did not have to think about how Ferdinand's agonized screams.

He did not have to think about the sound of metal teeth grinding against bone.

It was all music, in the end, was it not? Awful, discordant music.

He chose one of the ivory keys and stroked it with two fingers, allowing his touch to linger for a moment before crooking his knuckles and striking it in the smooth center. A single, ringing chord yelped as it was plucked. He felt it like a tightening wire wrapped around his heart.

The harpsichord whimpered again, although the second time was not his fault. Ephraim's shoulders jerked with surprise and he looked over, catching a glimpse of a familiarly gloved hand. Hester Primus' gloves, in particular, had always been unnecessarily gaudy—black leather stitched with silver across the back, intertwined with an elaborately embroidered red 'H'. Then, of course, not all of the fingers moved—on account of a few being fake, he was missing so many. Ephraim frowned and looked up, brushing his hand through his tumble of soft strawberry curls.

"I did not hear you come in," Ephraim said. Hester's scarred mouth twitched.

"I suppose that is what comes of driving piano wires into your ears," the sorcerer said, "It is a miracle you can hear anything at all."

Hester had a few distinguishing features—from the scar that cut across his face to his false gold nose—and that was all Ephraim had to cling to. Faces, otherwise, had a tendency to melt away into something unrecognizable. Which was unfortunate for many reasons, not the least of which was that it had become nearly impossible to read lips after a prolonged period.

The lye he drank after Ferdinand's death did not kill him, but it had corroded his insides.

Hester smashed the harpsichord keys again. Ephraim flinched.

"Master Holst." The way that Hester curled his dark, eel-like tongue around the name made it sound like he was trying to catch the attention of a child. "Are you entirely present?"

Ephraim drew in his breath and held it there, nodding. "I am," he said as he released it.

"The queen was disappointed by the lack of singing during the last banquet. She felt that it left the orchestra's performance overall...wanting." Hester crossed his hands over the head of his cane. "I brought to her attention that you have yet to replace your vocalist."

Ephraim's fingers twitched violently and he slid his hands into his pockets, hoping to contain them. "It has only been—"

"A month," Hester cut him off, "far more than is warranted." He gestured, and another body joined the fuzzy halo of Ephraim's vision. This one had fewer memorable facial features, but he caught a glimpse of brown eyes before they melted away. Auburn curls and warm olive skin, a smattering of dark freckles that vanished down the neck of a high, dark blue velvet collar. Decidedly human by the shape of the ears. Or, at least, human enough that the queen would allow them through the inner palace doors.

To Ephraim's sensitive nose, they smelled like lavender water, oranges, and cloves—royal baths and expensive fragrance oils. One of her castrati, more than likely.

"A soprano, then," he said, completing this thought aloud with nothing to explain how he arrived at that conclusion. He could not bite back his disgust in time to keep it out of his voice. "I can do nothing with a soprano. My..." he could not bring himself to say Ferdinand's name, "my...last soloist was a perfect tenor."

An irate sound churned in Hester's throat. "Are you a soprano, Amadeo?"

"Yes, my lord," the young man returned in a soft, well-tempered voice. "And a very great admirer of Master Holst's work. It is an honor to be brought to the Royal Music Master, especially when he is the foremost visionary maestro of the current age."

Nothing about his tone seemed insincere, which irritated Ephraim more.

"Yes, well." He turned his head. "My last vocalist had his head sawed off." His stomach churned over the words. "You are already missing some vital parts, and I would hate for you to lose another."

"I could propose a separate, and far more likely scenario," Hester said, "in which the Music Master gets hung upside-down with his bowels sliced open."

Ephraim's hands were starting to hurt more, and the pain distracted him from the threat. His desperation led him to wondering where he had left his braces. "Do you know anyone who can conduct an orchestra, Amadeo? Or play the harpsichord?"

"No," the young man said, sounding a little taken aback by the question. "Ah, I mean—no, master. I do not know anyone who can do such things."

"Well," Ephraim concluded, "it sounds like Her Majesty will *not* be hanging the Music Master anytime soon, then." He threw a look at Hester with as much venom as he could manage.

The sorcerer did not seem perturbed. "Her Majesty expects that she will hear singing during this evening's soiree," he said. "However you wish to make that happen, Master Holst, is up to you."

"I will bear that in mind." Ephraim raised his chin. "I am certain that you have better things to do, in the interim."

Hester made a sound of agreement. He turned away, his heavy fur pelt brushing Amadeo's shoulder as he walked past. The young man remained perfectly still, waiting until the sorcerer had left the room altogether before exhaling sharply—as if he had been holding his breath the entire time.

Once he was gone, the room was swallowed by oppressive silence. Ephraim would have been content to let it linger, but he was afraid that it would encourage the younger singer to speak up. Rather than endure small talk, he walked over to the harpsichord and flicked on the metronome that was sitting on its spine so that the silence was broken by its methodic ticking.

"All right, then," Ephraim began as he looked around the instrument for his braces. "Do you know anything? *Cazio's Lament? The Nightingale Chorus?*"

"Yes," Amadeo said with confidence. "And I know *Whistle on the Wind.*"

"That is a tavern song," Ephraim responded with disdain. He found his braces underneath the stool. He sat down to slip them onto his hands, grimacing as the silver bands pinched his skin. "Try another."

Amadeo considered. *"Morcant's Aria?"*

Ephraim bit the inside of his cheek and looked up, flexing his fingers and feeling the metal joints creak across his knuckles, even if he could not hear them. The braces were unpleasant, but at least his hands were no longer shaking as badly. "I should allow you to sing the tavern song," he scoffed. "At least that will not bore Her Majesty to sleep."

Amadeo swallowed. "I am sorry, master." He clasped his hands behind his back. "I can assure you that I am quick to learn."

"I am sure." Ephraim put his face in his hands, taking a moment to collect his thoughts. They spun around the inside of his skull, loose and faded spirits that completely evaded his grasp. Finally, after losing track of how long he had been sitting like that, he straightened his back and rolled his head around to pop his neck. He set his fingers against the keys—and though the braces kept them steady, there was nothing to stop his heart from plummeting into his stomach at the mere thought of playing *Cazio's Lament* for someone else. Ferdinand sang it so beautifully. Every star in the heavens would surely rain down in protest.

"Maestro?" Amadeo prompted him gently. Ephraim shook his head and looked up. His fingers were pressed down so hard against the keys that the harpsichord was screeching, and he did not know how long his hands had been in that position.

He opened his mouth to speak, and his tongue suddenly felt dry. He swiped it around the inside of his mouth and tried again, pushing a hand through his curls and narrowly avoiding getting them snagged on the braces.

"We will try *The Nightingale Chorus*," he said. "Of course, I will have to adjust it for a soprano."

Amadeo did not say anything, but he did move closer to the instrument. He set his hand gently against the wood, and Ephraim bit down on his own tongue to keep from snapping. His nostrils flared and he swiped one hand through the air, shooing the young man away from his instrument.

"Do not touch it," he said. "Sing, as you are meant to."

He did not give Amadeo a chance to respond, although he saw a flush climb up the young man's neck. Ephraim played the opening notes to *The Nightingale Chorus*, steeling himself for bitter disappointment.

From the moment Amadeo opened his mouth, it was all wrong. Even though every word was in Eastern Avralaenian, they were clumsy on his tongue. He butchered them with a heavy Western dialect. His voice was well-trained, but it lacked something *bright*. Sopranos were meant to sparkle, like bubbles in a champagne glass. His was smooth, and he hit every note—but it was uninspired. There was no beauty, no passion. Ephraim could hardly bring himself to bear the first verse before bringing it all to a halt.

"No," he said, his own voice quavering with fury. "No, no, not at all—not at all, that is no good. We are going to try it again. Can you sing? Can you, truly? Do you *believe* that you can? *Mi dhiegh*—please, tell me why the queen would send me a vocalist who cannot hit the top *trebasto* notes!"

Amadeo might have been choking back tears. Ephraim could not see his face well enough to tell. He saw a few droplets slip down the young man's chin before they were dashed away by his sleeve, and his voice sounded thick by the time he spoke again.

"Forgive me," Amadeo said, clearing his throat. "I will try it again."

"Again, again, but tears will ruin your voice—so, do not cry! Do better, *mi dhiegh*," Ephraim rubbed his face, the silver cold against his skin. Amadeo cleared his throat again and hardly had enough time to collect himself before Ephraim started the piece over. Amadeo began again, and Ephraim could tell that he was trying—but the only emotion evident in his voice was his own staggering sense of failure. The finer notes had been eroded by his tears, and where his voice had struggled before—it now fell entirely too short.

Perhaps the queen felt that such a devastatingly inferior voice was good enough for her Court High Aristocrats, but Ephraim was not willing to stake his reputation on a choked-up castrati when there were blind birds in cages who sang better from the corners of marketplace stalls.

"Enough, enough," Ephraim interrupted Amadeo again. "I cannot tolerate much more."

"Maestro," Amadeo's voice was soft, almost too soft for Ephraim to understand what he was saying. Somehow, that brought his frustration to a breaking point.

"*Speak up!*" Ephraim snapped. "If you are going to speak to me at all!" Amadeo jumped a bit, seeming a little startled, and touched the harpsichord again—although he pulled his hand back immediately, as if he had been burned.

"Maestro," Amadeo's voice was stronger as he repeated himself, "I have spent my entire life being trained to sing in court. Forgive me, the queen sent me to you because she knows that I *can* sing." He lifted his chin, emboldened by his own assurances. "The man who instructed me was also the man who leant his hand in fine-tuning Ferdinand Bauer's own golden throat—"

As soon as the words escaped his mouth, it was as if the young man sensed that he had said too much. He bit down on the last of his words, cutting them off unfinished and allowing the damning statement to hang limply in the air.

The phantasmal wire that was wrapped around Ephraim's heart tightened again. Any tighter, and he felt as though it would slice in half. He would collapse, dead, on the floor. He almost wished that it would. One more tug.

Instead, he stood. He stopped the metronome's pendulum mid-swing so that there was only silence between them again. The young man took a cautious step back, and Ephraim closed the distance quickly. Amadeo kept moving until his back hit the wall, narrowly avoiding the corner of a framed painting.

Ephraim pressed in until there was only a hair's breadth of distance between them. Up close, it was easier to pick up some details—those warm brown eyes floating across smooth nothingness before disappearing once again—a full pair of lips pressed so tightly together that they were quivering. They disappeared, too—yet despite being unable to stay focused on Amadeo's features, he kept his gaze fixed upon the blurry surface—if for no other reason than to watch the would-be soprano squirm.

Amadeo's chest rose and fell rapidly with every mounting, fearful breath. Now that they were so close to one another, it was clear how much shorter the young man was. Ephraim towered over him, aware of himself and how every inch of him was pure creature. He wondered if Amadeo found his eyes too unsettlingly yellow, or if the sharp points of his teeth were visible through his snarl.

"You had something to say, I believe," Ephraim said, flattening his hand against the wall beside Amadeo's head. "Do not let me interrupt you. Do you hold yourself in the same esteem as the name of Ferdinand Bauer?"

"No," Amadeo said quickly, "no, no, maestro. That is not—"

"It sounded like that was what you said," Ephraim lowered his chin.

"It is not what I meant," Amadeo's pulse raced in his jugular. It throbbed visibly—that much Ephraim *could* see. "I would never, I could never—no one could replace such a voice. No one could dare *try*."

Ephraim's head ached. His blood buzzed in his ears. His arm shook trying to support his weight and the tendons in his hand burned, but he did not relent. He rolled his head to pop his neck again, groaning at the ache that seemed eternally lodged in his spine.

"Right," he said. "No one would dare." With his free hand, he reached into his vest pocket and pulled out the silver penknife he always kept. It was a delicate little blade with a mother-of-pearl handle, but it was razor-sharp and had never failed him for use. He placed the tip against the soft part of the young man's chin, applying just enough pressure for it to be uncomfortable, but not enough to break the skin. "If Ferdinand's throat was made of gold, then yours is beaten copper. Gold is soft and they sawed right through it. Do you think he bled gold, when his head hit the boards?"

"I..." Amadeo's words faltered. "I know it did not, maestro."

"Speak up!" Ephraim bared his teeth. "Do you think he bled gold?"

"I know he did not!" Amadeo screamed. The penknife pricked his skin and blood ran in dark streams down his throat.

"Were you there?" Ephraim asked. "I was not. I was in the infirmary—I wanted to die before him, to be there to greet him at the Gates of Balam. Instead, I heard him scream, and I lived—even though I drank enough lye to kill a horse."

Amadeo whimpered. "Forgive me," he said, "please, maestro. I will go."

"It would take them a lot longer to cut off your head," Ephraim spoke as if he did not hear Amadeo's pleas. "They could not saw through your coarse, common throat quite as quickly. It took them half an hour with my beautiful Ferdinand," his own voice stuck, "It might take an hour for you. Perhaps two. You would make a far prettier sound suffering than you ever did singing." He finally pushed himself away from the wall, taking a step back while clutching his penknife. The world was spinning. He felt like he could collapse. He wondered if it showed, how he held his head and rocked on his heels.

Amadeo's entire body tensed as if he was ready to bolt. He pulled himself away from the wall and held up his hands, his cuffs stained with blood that was dripping from his chin.

"It should not have happened," the young man said. "What they did to Ferdinand—it was a pity. I was as surprised as anyone to hear of his treason."

It was too much. Ephraim clutched at his curls, gripping them by the roots with such ferocity that his scalp stung. Amadeo's voice was fading, and all he could hear were Ferdinand's screams. His screams, and the voice of Lord Loris—all the things he testified to the queen that were not true, that were simply not true.s

Ephraim screamed. He grabbed Amadeo by the hair and jerked his head back hard enough that he heard something crack. He swept his penknife in an arc, and any sound that the young man tried to make bubbled out with the blood that gushed from his open larynx. The would-be soprano made a few wet gasping sounds and stumbled forward. Ephraim pulled him back again to keep the blood from splashing on his red tights before releasing his grip and letting the young man fall.

Amadeo hit the floor, his temple bouncing off the polished marble. His hands scrabbled weakly, trying to gain some support, but there was too much blood, the surface was too slick. Mercifully, it did not take long for his hands to stop moving.

Ephraim looked down at his blade. Its silver edge glistened with droplets of blood like garnets. He bit his lip and pulled a handkerchief free from his cuff to drag over the knife.

"Are you alright?" Sopespian's voice was familiar to him, and clear enough that he could understand. Ephraim swayed on his feet, still dizzy.

"How much did you see?" Ephraim asked flatly.

"Enough," Sopespian said, "almost everything." He moved a little closer, extending his hand to Ephraim. The maestro took it gratefully, allowing himself to lean on the astronomer's arm.

"Her Majesty will be pissed," Sopespian said, "I can help you clean it up."

"I should let her execute me," Ephraim groaned miserably. "It is all that I have wanted since..."

"I know," Sopespian interrupted him. "That will not do any good, however."

"Why did you not stop me?" Ephraim asked.

Sopespian was quiet as he thought it over, and then he shrugged.

"I do not know," he said. "I did not think that you wanted me to."

Ephraim sighed. He leaned against Sopespian a little heavier.

"There is no way to prepare the meat," the maestro said, "not without being noticed."

"I know," Sopespian told him. "Worry about the blood, not the meat. If nothing else, Cahal likes to tear it from the bone."

Journal Entry

Concerning Cahal

THERE ARE A FEW very important things about Cahal that I must make clear. He and I were born into the same pod. I did not know him well or like him much, then. Of the two of us, he was captured first. I was brought to shore some months later, although time is not measured in the same ways below water, and it did not feel as though so much of it had passed at the time. When I was brought to the palace, Cahal advocated for my placement. Back then, there was only him and Hester Primus. I think he wanted to feel less alone. I would even venture so far as to suggest that he wanted a friend.

Over the years, we have developed something that is very like friendship where I find his faults to be equal amounts of infuriating and endearing. He is an immovable force of will, stubborn and brazen in the way that he never fails to speak his mind, even when it is to his detriment. He is a pit viper on the battlefield, and he does not tolerate disrespect from his subordinates. Too often he acts before he thinks, but it is his prowess in battle and his unmatched brute strength that keeps him in favor with Her Majesty.

He is her bull. He will go in whatever direction she turns him and will not come to heel unless she bids.

He is entirely at her command, which is his greatest fault. Though he has no love for her, his sense of duty is welded to his very bones like an iron cage for an untamable beast. The Queen has less control over him than she would like to admit, and at times I think she fears him.

There are many in courts both high and low that refer to him as 'Admiral Blood', and they say his hands are stained red. This rumor, I believe, is perpetuated by his constant wearing of gloves. Allow me to explain that.

Cahal was born with poison skin, as was I. It is not uncommon for naiads of our variety. Yet, for him, it is a source of shame. He will, and has, weaponized it often enough—but in a fury, or in the middle of a fight, and never with the finesse of an assassin or any shrouded intention. His skin is marked by two bright red stripes running over his right eye—what nature intended to serve as a warning. Yet, nature could not have done what Cahal manages to do for himself in order to keep everyone at arm's length. East Avralaenian fashion loves high collars, long sleeves, and long trousers. He has embraced this way of dressing with a few amendments of his own. I, his friend, have never seen him without gloves. When he leaves the palace, he keeps his bottom face covered with a bronze mask. There are ivory teeth affixed to this mask, and they jut out in every direction like an angler fish. Within the palace walls, he keeps to himself. He does not like to be touched or approached, not even by me, and knowing that I am immune. He always sits apart. He says he prefers it, although once he admitted that he has no way of knowing who among us he is capable of killing, and it is a risk he does not wish to take. He believes that he cannot be loved, and even if he could be, that he is undeserving.

There is no one who is more melancholy or full of self-loathing than Cahal.

Cahal

CAHAL

THE ADMIRAL OF BLOOD

T HE RHYTHM OF THE queen's cane as it swung through the air came in low, thrumming vibrations. Cahal could not tear his eyes away from the hypnotic motion of the blunt brass stopper as it moved back and forth like the pendulum of a clock. The carved wooden handle, formed to resemble a gryphon's head and worn to fit the grooves of her hand dangled from the ends of her needle-thin fingertips, the gentle bumps of which propelled the entire cane into motion.

It was easy, settling, to make her the center of his focus—despite how angry she was with him. He recognized the shrewd moue of her lips and the way her chin wrinkled as her displeasure. He kept his back straight and his shoulders squared, unbuckling, exactly as he had been trained. It was a waste, considering she was not even looking at him directly. The heat of her gaze sizzled past his shoulder, fixed on the bedraggled group behind him—humans who had seen better days. They stood in a line with wind-chaffed skin and clothes crusted with salt, their heads bowed low and lanky damp hair stuck to their neck like tendrils of kelp.

They would be dead soon, if they were fortunate.

The brass end of the queen's cane struck the marble floor and the sharp sound pulled Cahal from his reverie.

"Admiral." The queen's voice was clipped.

Cahal lifted his head. Late afternoon sunbeams streaming through tall arched windows bathed the throne room in an ethereal orange glow. The gilded throne itself cast a long shadow, stretched outward like the dark Hand of Morcant reaching for lost souls just out of grasp. Queen Robin Brahntaiste, swathed in yards of green and gold brocade and soaked in empyreal light, seemed more god revealed than elven ruler. If she would but give him reason, he would fear her.

"Your Majesty." He presented her title without weight or ramification behind it. He watched her mouth twist again, the corners deepening with irritation.

"Is this all that you have brought back for me?" Now that her cane was no longer in motion, the room had been swallowed by stillness.

"And the ship," Cahal said, "as well as the crew. I did as I was instructed."

"Four Grauel mages," the limits of Robin's patience were being reached and squeezed through the spaces of her teeth with every word, "that you have broken beyond repair."

Cahal raised his chin a little higher. "They cannot cast without their hands," he said flatly, "you said to bring them here. I did so."

"I was unaware that I needed to specify how I wanted them *whole,*" the queen snipped back. "Now your voyage has been wasted."

Cahal kept in a sharp exhale. It mingled with a hot flare of anger and burned deep in the cavity of his chest.

"That one," he offered as he tilted his head and indicated over his shoulder, "may be salvageable."

"I should hope so. For your sake, I do not want to be forced to hang them all."

Cahal's glittering red eyes caught the afternoon light and he pinned down the queen's gaze. "Next time you see fit to send me to the tip of the continent again, Your Majesty, have a care to be more specific. And bear in mind that unbroken mages and living crews do not necessarily coincide."

"You forget yourself, Admiral. Keep your tongue behind your teeth or your next trip around the continent will be on a funeral barge."

Even as she spoke, Cahal bit the tip of his tongue between his sharp incisors to curb any response that might tempt his fate. He bent at the waist, only as much as rectitude demanded, and took a step back as the queen dismissed him with a word.

The Grauel mage behind him stumbled as they tried to move out his way. Cahal felt his shoulder collide with the prisoner's and it was entirely on instinct that his gloved hand shot out to grab them by the wrist. They swayed on their feet for a moment, and he pulled them back towards standing upright. What remained of their ruined hands was bleeding profusely through thick bandages and he could feel the tackiness start to transfer to his gloves. Cahal's lip curled, his fingers tightening around the mage's wrist like steel bands. He heard the mage whimper just underneath the vicious snap of bone, which burst from their skin like the head of a spear and sprayed gore on Cahal's sleeve.

If anyone nearby said anything to him, it was lost over the roar of blood rushing through his ears. Cahal kept his gaze locked with the mage's, just long enough to see agony illuminate their grey eyes—a sudden sharp clarity that always came before the dull, glassy wave that never failed to wash all the color out. The human body tried its hardest, but it could never allay pain in the ways a naiad's could. It fascinated him as much as it made his teeth ache. Cahal gnashed them together to nip his hunger back, though the acrid scent of blood was enough to send a sharp pang through his stomach like a spear.

The mage's eyes flashed white. Cahal slackened his grip so that when they fell to the ground, they did not drag him down in the same motion.

He swiped at the bit of saliva that had started to gather in the corners of his mouth. He could feel the queen's eyes burning through the back of his skull, though that was easily enough ignored as he left the throne room altogether without bothering to resume protocol.

One was to never turn their back to the queen.

He would hear about it later, he was certain.

T HE STEPS LEADING UP to the astronomy tower were broad and uneven. The spiral staircase twisted in unnatural ways with some of the steps bulging and overlapping, resembling more of a monstrous growth than an architectural anomaly. The corridor itself became narrower as it progressed towards the top, and the steps became even steeper until they were nearly impossible to traverse. It all ended in a rotted wooden door, with barely enough left to cling to its stocky frame.

Cahal hated the climb, though he did not mind the tower itself at all. It smelled of mildew and mold, and there was moss on the very last few steps, but it had enough archer's slit windows that he could catch the salty scent of a stinging sea breeze; and because of its occupant, he knew he would never be followed.

Sopespian Slaine was exactly where Cahal expected to find him—hunched over the pages of a journal with his inky fingertips leaving smudges through his drawings. His eccentrically long legs were hooked around the rungs of the stool where he was sitting, and the hem of his maroon coat obscured them from view. On the ground beside him, Jules Vernon sat in a puddle of their own velvet robes—only immediately recognizable because of the flame-orange braid slung over their shoulder like a rope. Neither looked up, although Cahal could tell by the way Jules' pointed ears flicked that it was likely they had heard him.

"I despise the bitch," Cahal announced with a growl. Jules looked up at last and nudged Sopespian with their elbow.

"I think he is talking to you, dear," they said sweetly. Sopespian raised his head, although it took him a few extra moments to pull his eyes up from his work, and he looked at Cahal from over the rim of his monocle.

"Which one?" Sopespian asked.

Cahal aimed a kick at the door behind him. It made a dangerous splitting sound when it slammed back into place. "*The* bitch," he said, "the uncontested sole sovereign of the Titan Continent—I have thought kindlier of spurs trapped in my boots."

"Sole sovereign?" Sopespian adjusted his monocle. "I can think of at least two kings who might disagree with you."

"Piotr out West is completely under her thumb, we all know it," Cahal scoffed. "And in Graueyette, whoever that is—"

"Priapus," Jules provided.

"It does not matter. He cannot unseal his borders without fear that she will come crashing through the gates and take everything he has." He rubbed his face, raking his gloved fingertips down the bright red marks over his eye. "I am hungry," he finally admitted.

"I can tell." Sopespian nudged Jules with his leg and slipped off the stool. The astronomer was lanky and made a habit out of never standing straight. If he were to do so, Cahal would only come up to his chest. "Four mages marinating together in a cage were a real temptation, no doubt." He reached out, flicking his finger through the air over the corner of Cahal's mouth without touching. Cahal flinched anyway and grimaced, swatting at Sopespian's hand.

"You are drooling," Sopespian said. "I must not be far off the mark."

"How long has it been for you?" Cahal dragged his hand across his mouth, no longer looking at the astronomer.

"Ten days." Sopespian fussed with the lapels of his coat. "Are you thinking about a dive?"

"Maybe," Cahal said. "I am not off-duty for another hour."

"All things considered, I think you can duck out a little early." Sopespian placed his hand on Cahal's shoulder, squeezing it through the layers of leather and linen that shielded his poisonous skin. "Will you be joining us, Jules?"

"No," Jules said primly, still not having moved from their spot on the floor. "I have a meeting with Lord Loris in a while." They looked up towards the glass-domed ceiling that offered nothing other than blue sky and a few wispy white clouds, as if that was a far better indicator of the time than the pocket watch looped through their robes. "Will you be going to the Gold Gryphon?"

"To the King's Head, more than likely," Sopespian smirked. "I think Cahal is banned from the Gryphon."

Cahal snorted. "I doubt that they would bar me from entering."

"Queen's Admiral or not, you cannot break a clay dish over a man's head and expect to be welcomed back." Sopespian laughed. It was an odd, idiosyncratic sound. "Well, if that is what you must do, Jules. I will see you. Bolt the door when you leave."

"Is the bolt still attached?" Cahal asked dubiously. Sopespian shrugged and ushered him out.

IT WAS A FARTHER walk to the King's Head, but the ale was just as dark—if not darker—than at the Gold Gryphon, and they did not turn up their noses to brinefolk. During the warmest months, they kept their doors propped open with colorful stones and allowed the fresh air to sweep out the offensive smell of damp rushes, spilled beer, and sailors. So early in the day, there were only a few patrons hanging around—most of them travelers or regulars who were keen on getting an early tipple before the evening crowd swarmed in. Cahal did not mind a rougher tavern—he usually had no problem clearing a path through even the busiest crowds and finding himself a seat. Sopespian was the one who picked his way through, using his cane to seek out soggy spots in the rush mats and then stepping over them.

Cahal sat down first and ordered them both some mead.

"I ordered for you," he said when Sopespian finally joined him at the table. The red-haired astronomer brushed the crumbs off his chair before sitting down.

"How kind of you." Sopespian kept his cane by his side, distractedly sliding his gloved fingers over the round brass head. "We garnered a fair few more irregular looks than usual on the way here. Did you notice?"

"Somewhat," Cahal admitted as a barmaid set two tankards down in front of them.

Sopespian selected one for himself. "I wonder if they heard of your blunder with the queen."

"I doubt that anyone past the palace gates cares about that." Cahal rolled his eyes and swiped up the other mead. He cast a glance around the tavern, studying every singular body that was slouched at a table or bent over the bar. "What do you think, then? Anything promising?"

Sopespian darted his tongue over his lips. "I like the look of that one," he said, trailing his fingers through the air before wobbling the head of his cane to gesture. "Closest to the door."

Cahal turned his head. The man that Sopespian had singled out looked to be some sort of farrier or an equally rough trade. His large, grimy hands gripped his half-empty pint like a lifeline, and he quaffed its contents, pausing only every now and again to suck a breath through his nose. Cahal watched as the man was handed another pint and saw its contents vanish in under two minutes.

"He is not going to taste very good," Cahal said. Sopespian shrugged.

"A little bitter," he said, "the selection will only get worse as the night goes on." The tip of his tongue wet his lips again, and he swiped it back and forth for an indecisive moment. "You wanted to go on a dive, so I will allow you to choose the quarry."

Cahal shifted his back teeth. "Do you think that we can get him to the river?"

"Easier, I would say, than chasing him out towards the beach," Sopespian said.

"All right," Cahal muttered, draining the last of his mead. He had allowed his eyes to linger too long, and now he was turning the man over in his brain and dissecting him. The farrier's skin was a little ruddy, with sweat and dirt caking the creases in his skin. Yet, his cheeks were full, and his arms were large and sinewy—but there would certainly be more marbling further down the torso. There would be plenty to tear from the bones. Cahal had tasted worse.

His teeth ached and he rubbed the corner of his mouth. "Will you follow?"

"Of course," Sopespian reassured him.

Cahal stood and walked across the room. Now that he had his kill within his sights, it was difficult to think of anything else. He trusted Sopespian to keep any onlookers at bay. Most of the other patrons were too deep into their ale to notice anything unusual—and anyone who was aware of what was about to happen likely knew better than to interfere.

Cahal stopped at the table and the farrier looked up. It took everything Cahal had not to tear off his glove and wrap his hands around the man's throat. It was easier that way. The man's face would go from red to purple and the veins in his eyes would burst. Foam would pour from his mouth and he would fall down dead within moments—maybe a convulsion or two would tear through his body and knock him to the floor. Cahal held onto that imagery until his fingers twitched. He stroked them beneath his gloves, hoping the motion would settle his nerves.

Out of respect for Sopespian's sensitive stomach, and in the spirit of good sportsmanship, he would do things the hard way.

Cahal took a deep breath. He spoke in Brebble—the sounds that came out of his mouth closer to dolphin clicks and chatter than anything that could be recognized as a word in any human language. They had their desired effect—with the human man's head too steeped in ale to fight off their effect. Cahal did not know what he heard—every human picked out something different from the sounds—but it was enough to make him stand and drop his tankard. It smashed against the floor, but the barmaid did not even fuss. The room was quiet—although the only thing Cahal was focused on was the man's stupid face—his wide eyes, blown pupils, and his mouth hanging open like a fish.

Cahal jerked his head towards the door and walked out. The man followed him, heavy boots clunking like a draft horse. Cahal's heart raced behind his ribs, a mixture of anxiety and exhilaration from the hunt.

He was vaguely aware of Sopespian following him—and he only knew that by the smell of his perfume—which was faint, but Cahal's sensitive nose could place it anywhere. Cahal kept his eyes on the man in front of him, focusing on every stumbling step and encouraging him in Brebble. The city around him had become entirely light and sound and indistinct shapes—nothing mattered more than the kill.

Eventually, Cahal caught the scent of brackish water—and the sound of the churning river filled his ears.

The man came to the edge of the street and stopped. His boots shuffled over the raised stones uncertainly, grinding against the corner where the street turned into the bridge. He looked down at the water, balanced so poorly that he almost toppled without any prompting.

"Down there?" he asked, gesturing. Cahal nodded. He wanted to say something more, but he could not talk past his own tongue. It felt gummy and stuck to the roof of his mouth, despite how much he was salivating.

The man furrowed his brow, looking uncertain. He scuffed his foot over the edge of the raised stone and watched a few scattered pebbles fly towards the water.

Sopespian's voice barked something in Brebble, and the man paled. He pinched his nose and dove without another thought, his arms flailing, but he did not scream. He smacked against the surface of the water and sank like a stone.

Sopespian slipped off his coat and draped it over the bridge. "After you," he said to Cahal.

Cahal did not care about getting his own clothes wet, but he missed his brineskin. He watched the man sink for a few more moments, waiting until he was at a decent depth before diving in after him, sharp teeth bared to take the first bite.

A Letter to Cahal

With Express Regrets

*T*EXT TAKEN FROM A *crumpled letter discovered on a tavern table somewhere along the Dragolothian coast.*

My Dear Cahal,

That is as much formality as I can grant you. You and I, of all people, know the division that the pursuit of such stiff convenances can create. It is just as well that there is no genteel courtly ritual that will allow me to speak my mind. You may have expected me to write, and you may have even imagined the words I might say—gentle, entreating words full of soft longing, bent on wooing you to return. You should know by now that I have no such language reserved for you.

I am glad that you are gone. Of course, I will miss you. There is a deep hole left torn in all our hearts and it is in the shape of you. I understand that you left because you had no choice, but I do hate you, as well. There is resentment inside of me that boils at the thought of you and your lack of self-control. How selfish of a creature you are, to have let your own stubborn pride be your ruler. Without you, everything will fall into ruin.

I am glad you are gone, and I hope that you find freedom and happiness where you are. Jules sends their love and I send mine, even if I doubt that I will ever forgive you.

Remember that there is something worth fighting for, should you ever choose to return.

Your friend,
Sopespian

Journal Entry

On the Matter of Sweeney

I T IS AT THIS point that I will address a remarkable force of nature that has been sorely neglected in my narrative up until this point. There is a pirate by the name of Sweeney, known for one reason or another to be a proven terror on the high seas and a canker in the mouth of every monarch from here to Simisola. Though I have never met him, there have been several instances in which he and Jules have exchanged letters. From what I understand he is a proper scoundrel with a lustful appetite for gold, yet he has concerned himself more recently with a slave liberation movement that is making its way through Dragoloth. When these letters arrive, Jules always diverts them to their husband, and even my insatiable curiosity has not made me nimble enough to snatch one from their very capable hands. With that being said, I will chronicle what I know of the pirate and his exploits. If this entry holds any bad information, you may place your blame on Jules, as they are my only resource.

Sweeney is a siren, and that means he was not born with a brineskin. He has never been beholden to anyone other than himself, and he practices freedom in daring ways. His ship is fondly named *The Rooster*, and it is said to be lighter than foam while traveling faster than a whistle carried by a breeze. There are few who encounter him on the ocean and live to tell the tale. Of those who do return, they describe him as a rakish fiend, ill-mannered with a slick tongue and fingers that always stick to his cards. And yet, from those same mouths come the strained, stricken recollections of his voice. They can do little else except babble about how it supposedly rolls like thunder over the waves and throbs deep inside the hearts of men. Captains have returned to shore broken men, having lost entire crews to Sweeney's lure, and still their eyes will gloss over when they speak about those final moments—as if reliving a moment of perfect ecstasy rather than horror.

I have no reason to disregard these stories as there must be some truth rooted in them, yet I believe the deeds of this rapscallion speak for themselves.

It is abolitionist spirit that has propelled me to extend an offer of honorary membership to the Red Star Society. Though he is far freer than we are, and we could never be of much use to him, I believe that when the time comes he will prove an invaluable ally. I may write to him myself, one of these days. I do not doubt that, as a creature who spends so much time sailing, he has keen insights to offer about the stars.

Sweeney

SWEENEY

THE RAPSCALLION LIBERATOR

H E NEVER MET AN ale he did not like, and humans made it best. They liked it stiffer than a corpse and too dark to shine a light through, with just enough pale foam at the top to tickle their nose whenever they lifted their tankards. After decades' worth of dealings, Sweeney found that ales, meads, and the invention of shithole taverns were the one thing that men managed to get right. The rest was all dross. And their idea of food was not even worth a mention.

The man sitting across from him had already sent his bowl back to the kitchen twice. Each time it was brought back, the maid serving him looked increasingly nervous. Her hands shook whenever she lowered his bowl, and the watery contents sloshed around, dragging lumps of potato and mysterious hunks of—what could have been meat, at some stage of its life—towards the rim. Sweeney kept placing bets with himself about when it would finally spill, and every time he lost, he slipped a silver coin into the serving maid's apron when her head was turned. She never noticed, but the man across from him did. He regarded

Sweeney with tea-green eyes that looked like they were covered in a layer of dust. And there was nothing behind them; not a jot or spark of anything that might give the illusion of a personality. It was akin to staring down a lizard.

"So," the man said, "what do you think?"

Sweeney blinked. "I think that every time you send that soup back to the kitchen, it returns that much thinner. You will be lucky that they do not spit in it by the time you are satisfied."

"I meant in regards to my proposal," the man replied, and seemed to feel the need to add, "there is not a living soul who would *dare* spit in my food."

Sweeney thought about it. He pursed his lips, willing to chance the shot, but talked himself out of it just as quickly. He did not feel like bashing skulls with this dolt, who had under one minute to change Sweeney's opinion of the worthwhileness of their meeting.

"You said something about cargo across the Black Salt Sea." Sweeney racked his brain for any memory of their conversation before all the interruptions began. "To East Avralaen, I presume?"

"As a start," the man said. "East Avralaen's trading ports are the most prosperous in the world."

"So they say," Sweeney scoffed quietly. "And you seek to use my ship? Why?" He could not help a smirk that curled the corners of his mouth. "I am not the most honorable privateer."

"Nor are you just any pirate." The man tilted his head. "You and I are both aware of what they call you—*Den Blauefeall Drinnseet.*"

The Pale Blue Sea-Devil. Dragolothian's had a strange way of going about their words, and they liked to talk as if they had never seen a siren before. Sweeney stroked his chin.

"The cargo that I wish to negotiate is not conventional by any means," the man continued. "So I want a captain who will not turn up his nose at a pot of gold based on some prosaic moral standing."

"What is it, then? Pistols? Red?" The latter he had seen humans spill blood for. They took bricks of the stuff and chipped off pieces to melt down and inject in their veins.

The man held his gaze a little too long before saying the word, "Slaves."

Sweeney felt his expression shift, and he no longer cared what it looked like. He crossed his arms over his chest and leaned back in his chair, lifting his leg to rest against the round edge of the table. "What do you take me for?"

"A shrewd creature of business," the man said, "did I miss the mark?"

Sweeney darted his tongue over his sharp teeth. "It would seem that you do not know my reputation as well as you like to claim." He set his jaw. "I *burn* slave ships."

The man across from him did not flinch. "Until now, it has been more profitable for you to do so," he said. "Sink the ships, collect their bounty—gorge yourself on hearts, is that not what your kind enjoys?" The way he rolled his tongue around 'your kind' made the term sound deplorable. "There is more gold in running them across the water yourself—and we are not talking men, if that is the idea you so repudiate. I am not asking you to bite the hand that feeds you. What I bring to you will be sylphs." He paused, as if waiting for the gravity of his words to take effect. Sweeney only stared him down, hating him, and thinking about what his heart might taste like.

His nailbeds ached with the desire to tear into this man's chest. He flexed his fingers to try and ease the burn.

"Palace slaves, then," Sweeney had to shred the words through his teeth, "and stock for their brothels. You want to feed soft Dragolothian bodies to rowdy Avralaenian maws." On the scope of things, nationalities mattered very little to him—but there was a soft bruise of hatred on his heart for any Avralaenian, East or West.

"My slaves are kept pure for the discerning nobleman's household. They are well-trained and so obedient that they would rip out their own throats on a single command. They respond to whistles and hand signals. One need not even waste words on them." The slaver leaned in. "The bloody roots pulled from their scalp are worth more than ten whole men."

"A rather poor choice," Sweeney snarled, "for a man's last words."

The slaver raised his chin. "I can see that we will not likely come to an arrangement."

"Not likely," Sweeney's lip curled, "unless the arrangement is for you to be wrapped into your own chains and dragged down to the ocean floor. *That* I believe I could accommodate."

The slaver gave him another long look, as if he thought about saying something else and then decided against it. He turned his purse over onto the table and three silver dera rolled out, spinning on their thick sides until they fell.

Sweeney's yellow eyes darted down, tracking the gloved fingers that stopped the coins and slid them towards the center of the table. He spotted a gold signet ring with an elaborate 'E' stamped into the center. It looked like one he ought to recognize, but he could not place where he had seen it before.

"Suppose I change my mind," he said, trying to play it off as being moved by the display, "who should I call upon?"

"Pheseus Ercole," the slaver replied. "It is a well-known name. Should you go around asking for me, I have no doubt that we will find one another."

"I will count on that," Sweeney said. As the slaver left, Sweeney picked up his tankard and knocked back the rest of his ale, dragging his hand across his mouth to wipe away the foam.

THERE WAS NO POINT in dressing to go unnoticed—his river-colored skin betrayed his nature regardless of what he wore, and grandiosity was a part of his framework. The breeze that followed him from the dock raked its fingers down the tails of his crimson coat and snapped them playfully. Another color might have been better suited for chicanery, but he was not overly worried about being approached. Not by the people who whispered *den blauefeall drinnseet* and averted their eyes as they passed him on the street.

His crew member, Christiane, was a jot more concerned with their safety. He blended in a little better with his long black overcoat and his round wire spectacles that made him look like a clerk. He matched Sweeney's pace with the confident swagger of someone born into nobility, although Sweeney had known him since he was a boy, and knew he was just a downriver rat whose father traded pelts.

"My sources are good ones," Christiane said, with the air of someone who took doubt a little personally. "Pheseus Ercole is staying at the Red Horn." He pulled a folded piece of paper from his jacket and opened it up as they walked, smoothing out the creases with his thumb. "I have the room number, and a sketch that was made."

"It is uncanny," Sweeney said, "how you can acquire so much information so quickly."

"You just have to know where to ask," Christiane dismissed.

"What else were you able to find out?" Sweeney ducked underneath a low-hanging clothesline as he made a sharp turn down an alleyway. Christiane pivoted on his heel and kept up with him without missing a beat.

"About his family, or about his trade?" Christiane asked.

"What do you think?" Sweeney tsked softly. "I do not give a flying fig about his family."

"He will not have very many with him without a ship lined up to take more," Christiane said. He seemed to be having trouble over his words, an observation Sweeney made as he remembered, a little late, that such things might be a sensitive subject for a boy with a half-sylph mother. "He will have two, maybe three. He is the sort of slaver to collect as he travels and does not usually take on more than a handful at a time. The most he has ever been seen with was fifteen at a slave auction in Kantervale, and that was with a partner."

"Two of them?" Unhappiness twisted Sweeney's mouth.

Christiane nodded and pushed his glasses up the bridge of his nose. "You are going the wrong way," he interrupted himself to say.

"I am going the right way, I just do not want us to be followed," Sweeney said. "As you were saying—two, maybe three sylphs on hand? That is better than nothing. We can manage that."

"He turns around and sells them so quickly, and at such a high price, that it makes up for the lack." Christiane paused and added, lowering his voice as they slowed down, "Often such sylphs have either been taken and traveled far, or they have been sold by their own relatives, and either way they cannot return home."

"There is room on the ship," Sweeney said, "we can take them where they want to go." He held out his arm and stopped them at the mouth of the alleyway which emptied out onto the muddy street and gaped in the face of the Red Horn Inn. Of all the places for Pheseus to board, this one made the most sense—it was an obscenely expensive stay, and for no reason at all. The most it had to offer was a view of the docks, which you could get a full street over and pay far less. But then, he would have to be faced with the smell of sailors and tavern songs being sung into the late hours, and Sweeney had a notion that Pheseus did not mingle in any area that reeked more rancidly than his character.

"They may not *know* where they can go," Christiane said, stooping his shoulders to stay in the shadows and following the line of Sweeney's gaze. "The seas are rough. Our lives are rougher. Do you think that they can...?"

"By Tieres." Sweeney rolled his eyes. "We will *make* room. We always do."

Christiane shut his mouth and darted his tongue across his teeth. Sweeney saw the bulge against his sealed lips even in the dark. "You go, I follow."

"We will stick to what we discussed," Sweeney said. "I want you to go in and see if he is downstairs. If you see him, approach him, and act as thought you are my—"

"Envoy," Christiane supplied.

Sweeney nodded. "I will count to ten and wait. If you do not come back out, then I will know that you have found him. And I will climb upstairs." His yellow eyes were already scaling the side of the building, surveying the painted white trellis and the iron balcony that wrapped around the upstairs windows.

"You cannot see the numbers on the room from out here," Christiane said dryly.

"I think I will know which one is his," Sweeney said. "Your only focus is to make certain that he does not turn his head for any reason."

"Simple enough," Christiane said. "I am proficient in stroking a man's ego."

Sweeney's dark eyebrows bounced, but he did not make any salacious implications out loud. He patted Christiane's shoulder and his crewmate straightened. Christiane took a deep breath and his expression shifted. He might as well have pulled a mask over his face. He ran his fingers down his collar and touched the cravat around his throat—he looked like he could be a gentleman of modest means, in his stolen coat and affected airs.

He glanced down the street and then darted across, his low heels splashing in the puddles that had gathered from the afternoon's rain. Sweeney watched him disappear into the Red Horn and waited a beat before crossing as well, making his way, instead, to the darkness on the other side.

He kept an eye on the door, but he was not overly concerned. While theft was preferred, he was not above knocking a slaver down if he had to. Although, since he had just dropped anchor only a few days prior, he was not eager to gather up his crew and have them set sail, without proper rest or supplies, just to avoid a noose.

There were some, like dear Christiane, who were not as slippery or as quick as he was. And Sweeney did not want to lose any one of them.

The trellis was a little shaky. Sweeney grabbed hold of it through the holes and gave it a jostle—enough that the vines shivered, and it started to pull away from the wall. He decided that he was not willing to trust it with his weight. He took off his gloves and stuffed them in his pocket, trailing his hands over the brick to search for anything loose or missing that he could grab onto. His boot collided with the edge of something wooden, sending a shock of pain through his foot. Sweeney growled and looked down, his irritation quickly fleeing at the sight of a few stacked crates. That would be enough, then, to get him where he needed to go.

With light steps, he jumped up onto the crates and then jumped again to grasp an iron baluster. He swung for just a moment before he pulled himself up and set the toes of his boots against the balcony's edge. Sweeney hoisted himself over the railing and landed on the other side. The structure shivered underneath his boots, but other than that—he made it without a sound.

He paused for a moment to wait and listen for the sound of Christiane's voice. He did not hear anything, so he assumed that all was well. Sweeney turned his attention to the windows.

Most of them were dark. He flitted past a few, peering inside all of them just to be sure. The bodies that he could see were all asleep. Of the ones with lamps still burning behind them, the bodies inside were engaged in ways that he was not keen on observing. He began to regret his choices and wished he had started from the inside, as Christiane suggested.

The last window was dim. There was only a candle burning beyond the soft linen curtain. Sweeney stopped and glanced inside, thankful for the edge that his yellow eyes gave him against the darkness. Inside, he could see the shadows of two bodies—and more importantly, he could hear the rustle of iron.

Sweeney tapped his nail against the glass. The noises coming from inside stopped. He tapped again, and this time someone came to the window. The curtain slid away and there stood a sylph—all soft brown hair and large brown eyes—looking up at him with their mouth hanging open.

They clamped their hand down around their mouth and backed away from the window. Sweeney exhaled, the puff of breath that fogged the glass betraying his weariness. He crouched down and pulled a file from his boot, jamming it against the windowsill. The window popped up without much coaxing.

He was afraid that the sylphs would scream, but neither of them said a word. They stared at him with wide, watery eyes while clasping each other's trembling hands. The chains he had heard were finer than he expected and were linked to iron collars circled around their tender throats.

Sweeney fought to keep his anger down, not wanting to frighten the pair. He smiled, careful not to show his teeth.

"*Gottsvolden.*" He swept a bow. "Captain Sweeney, at your service."

The sylphs looked at one another and then the brown-haired one stepped forward, although they still did not let go of each other's hands.

"Did our master send you?" they asked. Sweeney pursed his lips.

"Absolutely not," he said. "In fact, he does not know that I am here at all. So, if you could refrain from calling out to him, I would be very obliged."

The brown-haired sylph drew in a breath, as if they were considering that very course of action. "What do you want?" Their voice shook, but he admired their acumen.

"To set you both free," he said, holding up the file. "I will help you get out of here, and you can join me on my ship, if you wish. That, or my crew and I will take you wherever you wish to go."

They did not look as though they believed him. The brown-haired sylph glanced over at their companion, worry knitting their fine brow.

"You are a naiad," the brown-haired one said. "You eat hearts."

"Yes," Sweeney said, "but not yours." He held up the file a little higher. "We do not have much time."

Both sylphs still looked a little doubtful.

"Why?" the second one, a blond, asked.

Sweeney waved his hand. "We can philosophize later," he said, "on the ship."

They exchanged another look and then the brown-haired sylph stepped forward, releasing their companion's hands. Sweeney slipped his fingers underneath the first sylph's collar and coaxed their chin upward with his thumb to keep it out of the way. He could take care of the collar itself on the ship. It would take longer—the chains would not be as difficult. They were attached by a simple ring.

He sawed through the ring and caught the chains before they clattered to the floor. Now that he had the enslaved sylphs in front of him, he was nervous about bringing too much attention their way. He had faith in Christiane's ability to keep anyone talking for an inordinate amount of time, but he was not keen on pressing their luck.

He beckoned the second sylph forward and cut through their ring in the same way. Once both were free, he drew them over to the window and glanced out. There was no one in the streets, but he had a feeling that that would not last long once the taverns started closing down for the night.

"All right," he said. "How good are either of you at climbing?" Flinging them off the balcony and hoping for the best was a last resort, but not off the table entirely.

"We have no shoes," the brown-haired sylph said. Sweeney nodded.

"Probably for the best." He slipped through the window and turned around to help them out. He waved towards the trellis, which—in his mind—they stood a better chance on than they would swinging down like imps.

"I will be on the ground first," he said with surety. "I will catch you if you fall."

They did not seem so sure of his plan, but he did not give them time to think it over. Sweeney cleared the balcony railing again and swung down the side, landing on the stack of crates and jumping down each one in rapid succession so as not to smash any.

He caught sight of Christiane as soon as he made it to the ground. His crewmate hissed through his teeth and waved him over. Sweeney raised his hand in acknowledgement and moved to stand underneath the trellis.

"We have to go," Christiane whispered when he was close enough, "I left him at his table, but the Red Horn is closing for the night."

"We are almost there." Sweeney lifted his arms, wiggling his fingers to encourage the sylph on the trellis to jump down. They looked uncertain, but they released their hold, and he caught them on their short descent.

"Two?" Christiane looked up.

"Unless he has another stashed underneath the bed." Sweeney held out his arms for the next. "What did he say to our generous counteroffer?"

"We can go to Balam, in no uncertain terms," Christiane said dryly.

"Wonderful."

Once both sylphs were on the ground, Sweeney grabbed the nearest one's hand and Christiane grabbed the other. The pirate's heart pounded with anxiety that he did not know he could possess.

"Where are we going?" With the addition of Christiane, the brown-haired sylph's voice sounded caught in their throat.

"To *The Rooster*," Sweeney said. "We will figure out the rest from there."

"You will be safe," Christiane reassured them. "Our crew believes strongly in liberation."

The young sylphs went quiet, which Sweeney preferred. The less they all spoke, the better their chances of making it back to the ship in one piece.

Journal Entry

The Enduring Brightness of Jules Vernon

THERE IS SO MUCH to be said about Jules Vernon. Ours was a fated match from the beginning. I must confess that I was not aware of their existence for the first few months. They squirreled themselves away so effectively in their library (an addition to the palace that I had no reason to frequent during that time) and remained hidden behind their stacks and shelves. They sorted everything out, beautifully, and it was only chance that I walked in on the very day that they shelved the last book. I caught them in a giddy state, dancing around and sipping tea as if it were wine, dancing in and out of the sunlight patches created by the large windows.

They flew into me before either of us could fully register that there was another person in the room. They spilled tea on my coat and they apologized, but not too sincerely, considering I was the one in their way.

From there, I have found myself bound in every way—heart and soul—they have my loyalty, as much as I can give, and my love—in what limited ways I am able to provide it. We were never meant to be romantic, and I do not believe that either of us has felt like we should try. I do not exaggerate, however, in saying that I would put up my life for theirs.

I digress. Yet, I give no apology.

Jules, Jules...they are clever and bright. They employ a wicked tongue as an agent for their sharp wit. There is nothing that occurs within the walls of this palace that misses their attention. They are beautiful, of course, with large round eyes that appear hopeful and naïve and sparkle under any light. They have deceived many men to ruin with such eyes. They possess a disarming sort of smile and an easy, forgiving nature that encourages one to confess their deepest secrets. Although, I will tell you, I find that there is very little about Jules' true nature that could be considered forgiving. They are not the sort to overlook a slight, nor are they one to forget. Jules has the patience of a saltwater crocodile, willing to wait for the opportune moment to snap.

Am I immune to their enchantments? Absolutely not. Have I tried to be? Certainly, no.

It was not long ago that Jules was appointed by the queen as the Master of Spies. That was her true intention all along, to put those dewy eyes and that playful smile to selfish use. However, the library is their true vocation, and knowing this she dangles it as an impetus to keep them compliant to her wishes. Jules does not resent the position so much as they find it disagreeable to be told what to do. In that way, they are the antithesis of Cahal, although they possess a great deal more power and are therefore, in my opinion, more of a danger to the queen than her mulish warmonger.

Jules has a little magic to them, as well, in a more literal sense. They have apprenticed themselves to a wizard who gifted them a magical tome. They tell me that this tome can do wondrous things, although I have yet to see it for myself. I do not know what business Jules wishes to have with wizards, especially one indentured to the queen, but I do not intend to hinder their pursuits.

Jules is an invaluable member of the Red Star Society. Their gumption, guts, and initiative keep us moving forward. We clash only on a few matters, the greatest among them being Hester's involvement. Jules hates Hester Primus with a passion so prodigious that, should a mortal man try to bear even half its weight, he would be crushed underneath it. And while I also despise Hester, I find myself constantly begging Jules' understanding. If Hester were not present, even as just a formality, he would raise such cane and create such havoc that not only would we be disbanded, but we would also be annihilated. He would see it done.

They are willing to placate me, for now, although I do not know how long that will last.

Even so, Jules is the center of my softest thoughts on rainy afternoons.

Jules

Jules

The Scholar of Ruin

THERE WAS MORE TO the palace library than record tomes and volumes of literature that the queen did not approve of. The pale lemon-yellow walls were lined with shelves upon shelves bearing the weight of centuries' worth of knowledge and stories. There were poems and books penned by writers long dead, bound in rich leather and cloth and left to rot on rigid white boards where no one could read them, no one could love them. Although there were no restrictions on who could enter the library, the Court High Aristocrats held little interest in anything that would force the cogs in their brains to turn a half quarter inch more than necessary, and anyone in the lower courts or below could hardly read at all. The Brahntaiste Reign had done its best to stamp out generations of progress and limit reading altogether, touting it as a luxury for the rich and a tool for those who could afford the education. And so, while there had been a great surge in innovation for manuscript printing and binding, its uses were severely hampered both by the crown's lack of imagination and its lust for control.

A notion which Jules could not bear to linger over unless they were willing to turn themselves inside-out and work themselves up into a frenzy. East Avralaen had the best of everything (so they claimed)—the most lumber, steel, labor, and gold—and yet, there were countries across the sea (on continents half the size!) where even farmers knew how to spell.

Jules had become accustomed to intrusions being limited to Her Majesty's evening events, when nobles would stagger in completely arse-over-tits and find a chair or a divan to fall face-down into and sleep off their champagne. Otherwise, the parlor was for gambling, and the drawing room was for heated political debates. Whenever the librarian complained, the queen would remind them that there were far more important matters to attend to—that the library was only under Jules' jurisdiction as disbursement for their services as Royal Master of Spies. She had a habit of referring to the library—in that haughty, condescending tone—as 'the conspiracy chamber' because of how well the open passageways and arched ceilings conveyed sound. Even the lowest whisper in the farthest corner of the room could be heard if one was listening from the right place. There were no muttered words or notes tucked between pages that Jules Vernon did not know about.

It was why she did not consult them when it came to certain matters—such as Ferdinand Bauer's supposed treason, or Cahal Ivers' mishandling of certain prisoners. Jules knew everything, and the queen was never interested in the truth.

And if she had asked them, even once, they would have handed her a list of Lord Loris' proclivities longer than her arm. But Loris had a father with more influence than any three members of the Queen's Chamber stacked together. The auburn-haired darling and pivot of upper society could not be publicly denounced as a wretch.

It was just as well, then. She had no way of knowing that Jules and Loris had been exchanging notes for months.

Jules knew that Loris favored a particular volume of poetry for his rendezvous. The book was white cloth with soft pink flowers and faded lettering, and it was kept tucked at the end of a very long shelf that ended where the entire structure conjugated with a corner. It was easy to overlook and impossible to care about. Loris left his perfumed notes wedged in the center, so that the person they were meant for could come by the library at some later hour and discover them. They would leave another in response and replace the book on the shelf—and so it went. It had not been difficult to intercept. Jules took out the note that had been left for Loris and replaced it with one of their own. The other they crumpled up and threw into the fire.

When Loris came, he seemed surprised, yet enthusiastic—nearly captivated. As Jules knew he would be.

And so soon after Ferdinand's death. It was nauseating.

Loris' letters had become too long to leave clamped between the pages of a small volume of poetry. He began to leave them in the tight spaces between books, where Jules could only find them by pulling out one book and letting the letter fall. The librarian never increased their own verbosity. They kept their notes flirtatious and succinct.

Just enough to entice, and they knew that it drove Loris wild.

The last note they left was only two words. '*Meet me.*' It was gone the next morning and nothing was left in its place.

When night fell, Jules drew all the curtains in the library and allowed the fire to sink low in its hearth. A little warmth was still pleasing, but less light was certainly preferred. Jules left a single lamp burning on the low center table and doused the rest, leaving every book-filled corridor cast in shadow.

An hour passed after sunset and then a little more, according to the hands of the small wooden clock that rested on the fireplace mantle. Jules waited in his favorite chair, turning the pages of his favorite personal tome. It was filled with Sopespian's drawings and notes, squeezed into the margins and invading the corners of Jules' otherwise pristine handwriting. It brought them some comfort and helped quell the anxiety that was beginning its vile surge up their throat.

Jules heard the library doors close, and they waited a moment before standing. When they reached the fireplace again, Lord Loris was standing in front of it, his arm resting against the mantle and a self-satisfied smile scrawled over his cattish, winding lips.

Jules paused and took him in, tilting their head in a slight acknowledgment. "Lord Loris," they said. "You honor me with your presence."

Loris played the part well—he was every bit an aristocrat. His auburn hair held streaks of gold and draped around his shoulders in perfect twin plaits that started at his crown and ended in long spirals. There were pearls strung throughout—so many courtiers had taken to wearing pearls since what they had all deemed *The Age of the Tide* began. When the queen started pulling naiads to her shores, the entire court had been overtaken by a fever. What they sickeningly referred to as *brine fever* cheekily amongst themselves. Pearl strings in their hair, exotic fish with every meal, rings made from sea glass—perfumes from naiad oils, leather from naiad skin—charms made from naiad bones.

Loris snapped his fingers, bringing Jules out of their distracted thoughts. He had blue iris eyes that possessed a disarming downturned shape. One had to look closely, and through such thick black lashes, to see that there was no warmth behind them.

"Are all naiads so easily distracted?" Loris spoke slowly and emphasized each word as if he was speaking to a foreigner. That grated on Jules' nerves, but they let it go.

"Only the ones I have met," they said. They moved a little closer, filling the silence with the sound of their velvet robes brushing against the floor. Loris' eyes followed them, and up close he was betrayed by the glistening corners of his mouth and the way his larynx bobbed with a hard swallow. No amount of poise could cover, entirely, the reason he had come. The carefully crafted tension that had been mounting between them for months was palpable.

Jules smiled.

"Well then, my lord," they lowered their voice demurely, "I see that you received my note."

"Verily," Loris breathed, "every single one." He reached out to touch Jules' hair, twisting an orange lock around his finger. "I would have kept them, if propriety and secrecy had not forced me to burn them."

"Of course," Jules said, "I understand."

"You can imagine my surprise when I discovered that you knew my secret," Loris continued. "And yet, rather than turn me over to the queen, you used it to your advantage. That was clever. Who knew that a little creature, such as yourself, was capable?"

Jules' smile was becoming more forced. They hoped that the darkness concealed its nature. "There are many rumors about brinefolk," they said, allowing the words to slip out on an intimate breath. "And simply none of them are true."

"None?" Loris purred. He brought his hand up higher to touch Jules on the cheek, sliding his finger up the line of their jaw and over their pointed, jeweled ear. "There are those who say that naiads are sexless—that your numbers are dying because you refuse to couple."

Jules' stomach turned. They leaned into the lord's hand.

"They deem us sexless because they do not want us—*coupling*, as you say—with anyone within the courts. Can you imagine how that would be?"

"I can imagine it," Loris said, moving closer until there was nothing more than fabric between them. "With ease."

Jules took a deep breath. They made certain that he could feel the rise and fall of their chest, the quickening pulse that he might mistake for thrill. "I have wine," they said, placing their hand against his chest. "Will you imbibe with me?"

An impatient look flitted across his face, but Jules did not wait for an answer. They backed away, and with the separation came a rush of urgency. Wine would only buy a little time.

Yet, there was something they had to know before all was said and done.

They led Loris to the divan. He took his seat and watched as they filled two glasses with sparkling strawberry wine—East Avralaen's most coveted prerogative. Jules passed him a glass and kept one for themselves, sitting close enough on the divan that their legs could still touch.

Loris raised the glass to his nose and sniffed it incredulously. "Champagne is the current fashion," he said.

"And yet, wine is favored by the queen." Jules lifted their glass. "To her health."

"To yours," Loris drank. Jules watched him drain his glass and then grabbed the bottle to refill it. There was more than enough—although the young lord was an infamous lush.

"Do you prefer champagne?" Jules asked conversationally. The young lord waved his hand dismissively.

"It is giddier than wine," Loris said, "and does not have the solemnity of brandy. Nor the rowdiness of rum—I have seen far too many good men lose their reputations to a rum bottle."

"As have I," Jules agreed. They crossed their legs, keeping their eyes on the lord's glass. When he drained it the second time, he held it out again, and they refilled it.

"I prefer to be giddy," Loris continued.

"I will have to bear that in mind," Jules returned. They set their own glass down, untouched, on the low table. "Ferdinand Bauer favored blackberry wine; I believe. Fresh off the coast of Dragoloth, imported all the way overseas." Even speaking the name threatened a sudden swell of grief, but they batted down the tears that pricked the backs of their eyes.

"I remember," Loris said, sounding somewhat reminiscent. "And I remember thinking that it was just like him—to be so spoiled. Every stroke the celebrated *v' fontadóire.*"

"It was earned," Jules said. "His praise, and his reputation."

"Every part." Loris took another deep swallow of wine. "It is a pity that..." he trailed off. Jules waited to see if he would say more and slid their own glass across the table as an offering.

"That...?" they prompted. Loris wiped at the corners of his mouth and picked up their glass, nearly draining it as well in three gulps.

"It is nothing you would know." The lord waved his hand again.

Jules shrugged. "Try me," they said.

"Well," a smirk pulled across Loris' lips, "allow me to confess that there is *one* rumor that was true—Ferdinand did, in fact, have a golden throat."

Jules wound their fingers into their robe and squeezed. "Oh?" They tilted their head naively. "Well, yes, he sang for every feast."

Loris laughed and shook his head, as if his cleverness was lost. "I believed another for a long time—that brine-folk choose one partner and stay with them for life."

"We do. That much is true," Jules said. "And once we choose our mate, most are unfalteringly loyal."

"*Most*," the lord said.

"There are a few who stray," Jules shrugged. "That is true of anyone—naiad or human. Although, I daresay, perhaps fewer in naiads than in lords."

Loris bristled, although he was too inebriated to take too much offense. He leaned over and picked up the bottle of wine by its neck, bypassing either glass altogether. "A truth that I was disappointed to discover."

Jules searched his face, trying to pluck out the answer before the man lost his ability to form words altogether. "You were in love with him?"

"Marriage was beyond us in these times, in this country—I courted him."

"He had Ephraim," Jules said.

Loris scoffed. "It is not a difficult sum to work out. I could have given him far more—I *gave him* far more—than Ephraim ever did. With me, he drank fine champagne and snorted Glow, and we spent hedonistic nights in ecstasy under the stars and in the waves on the beach. Ephraim could never bring his insufferable, orthodox self to compare."

"So," Jules said flatly, "he is dead—because your vanity suffered?"

Loris looked up. The last of his gusto had flown out with his words, and now his eyes were glassy, and his movements were sluggish. There was a white crust along the edge of his lip where he had drunk the wine so far down that some of the undissolved powder from the sleeping draught had washed onto his mouth. The bottle slipped from his hand and Jules caught it before it hit the floor, setting it down on the table.

"My vanity..." Loris muttered thickly. He stared at the bottle, and then back at Jules. "It is hard to breathe."

"Lie down," Jules said with thinly-veiled impatience. Loris began to obey, and would have fallen off the edge of the divan if Jules had not reached out to help. They rearranged him until he was comfortable and then pulled out a handkerchief to wipe away the wine and remnants of powder.

"It is still hard," Loris said. Jules pursed his lips.

"It will get easier," they told him. "It is just because you are falling asleep so quickly." They straightened and then turned to clean up the wine bottle and glasses. They took the time to carry them down to the kitchen and when they returned, Lord Loris was fast asleep.

Jules closed the library doors behind them, once again, and made their way over to the divan. They stood behind it, looking down at Lord Loris as they thought about everything he had said. Ferdinand may have been at fault for his wandering eye and his changeable heart, but it was nothing worthy of his fate. The accusations of treason, the trial that had dragged on for days, and his gruesome death—all brought upon them because a human lord, who could (and was known to) have anyone he wanted, felt jilted. It was more than an injustice, in Jules' mind. It was an atrocity.

It was proof that no matter what titles the queen bestowed upon her naiads or what favorable and mystic positions she granted them—they could be murdered, at any time, on any whim.

Loris' breathing was even. He smelled like wine, even from a distance.

Jules fingered the gold chain around their throat and slid the pad of their thumb all the way down to its end. From the depths of their velvet robes popped a charm—a beautifully engraved cone with a gold stopper in the shape of a gryphon. They held the charm up to the dim light, just enough to reassure themselves of the dark green liquid that was sloshing around inside. Satisfied, they pulled out the corner and lowered themselves over the back of the divan. Their long orange hair served as a curtain, preserving the final intimacy of the moment. They placed the cone against Loris' ear and tilted it onto its side. Poison filled the dark cavity and lingered in a pool before slowly draining down. Jules emptied more than half the bottle and waited until it had all disappeared before replacing the cork and dropping the necklace down their robes again.

They dabbed their soiled handkerchief against Loris' ear, sweeping up any final traces of poison. They wished that they did not have to sacrifice their divan to the cause, but the queen would surely have it replaced once the body was discovered. To even the most discerning physician, it would look as though the lord with no secret love of champagne and Glow powder had succumbed to too much of both.

If they were to crack open his head and investigate, as Jules knew no one would, they would find the insides completely black—as if his brain had been set on fire and torched the inside of his skull. His stomach and all his bowels would be black as well, reduced veritably to liquid.

The fire had died completely. The only source of light remaining was in Jules' lamp. They picked it up and set their hand against the curved glass covering, savoring the warmth that emanated through.

"I hope you meet The Voyager," Jules' scathing whisper cut through the darkness. "I hope that He drowns you in the River Balam and that your soul is lost before it hits the gates."

The hour was late. Loris had taken up far more of their time than they had designed. And there was still so much to do.

Jules made their way out of the library, and they left the doors open behind them. After all, they had nothing to hide.

A Letter to Jules

In Regard to Aurelius

*T*EXT TAKEN FROM *A letter discovered in the royal library, neatly folded between the pages of a tome.*

My Dearest Jules,

When I say that I do not know what has possessed you—I mean that sincerely. Over our many years together I have come to trust your judgment, and it is not until now that I find the very foundation of my faith in your usually reliable common sense shaken.

It was a mystery to me, at first, why you might be avoiding me. It has been three days since we have spoken. I was willing to chalk it up, at first, to Lord Loris' recent passing. You had something to do with it—I know you, and you are clever. I thought you might be keeping your head down in case the queen decided to pry into your affairs. Now, I understand! It does not have anything to do with Loris. Or, if it does, his involvement is so miniscule that it is hardly worth counting.

I know that you are smarter than this course of action might lead someone to believe. I, not being most people, can understand that we all experience deep lapses in judgment. And I do not know what led you to this desperate action, but as your friend, I must implore you to come visit me once more. Seek counsel and, by The Voyager's breath, do not try to shoulder this yourself.

Rest assured, my friend, that I am not here to berate you. I feel the need to provide you with information about this creature you have shackled yourself to hand-and-foot so that if you must proceed, you may do so with caution. I am aware that you might perceive this lecture as uncalled for, considering your position as the Master of Spies—yet, considering *also* your recent course of action, I intend to act as though this information was somehow neglected by your department.

This harpy, Aurelius, is the one that they call 'the Executioner'. He is an unyielding mercenary who will accept any job for the right price. He does not observe our rules of camaraderie, although I have no record—*yet*—of him slaughtering one of our own. You may be the first, if you venture too closely. There is a price on his head worth an obscene amount of gold. Was that all part of the allure?

I pray, I pray, that you will come to me and give your reasoning. It is not like you to keep such secrets from me.

Know that I care for you. It is out of love that I express my concerns.

In all sincerity,
S.

Aurelius

Aurelius

The Merry Executioner

THE DRUNKEN EGRET SMELLED like the river it stood next to: a unique blend of spoiled fish and rotting sewage, smothered in the bready smell of beer and a heavy fog of tobacco. Here, the ale was always watered down, and drugs traded hands as casually as currency. Glow, Red, opium, or tobacco—every vice, if it could be named, found its way through the swinging front doors.

Aurelius considered it his home. No one challenged him here. It was a shit-stain smeared across the map, but it sheltered him and his men when they needed it, and it always made certain their bellies were full. The owner was a short, busy sylph with a temper like fire on gunpowder. He could hardly be bothered to sweep the floors—far less was he worried about a handful of thieves.

Aurelius leaned over the table where he was sitting. A fine line of white Glow powder trailed across the copper plate in front of him and he cut through it with the edge of his knife, dividing it a few more times before scraping it back together and forming it into another line. He tested its grit by dipping his fingertip into the pile and placing what it collected against his tongue. The drug was too bitter to bear swallowing, but it dissolved quickly on his tongue and left nothing objectionably hard behind. Satisfied, he spat onto the floor to wash the taste out of his mouth. Aurelius pinched up a fair amount and piled it onto the bent knuckle of his opposite hand. He raised his hand to his nose and sniffed twice, once for each nostril, breathing in the Glow without a twitch. He never made a face, no matter how much it burned going up.

A body that he recognized as one of his men landed in the chair across from him and slammed a tankard down in the same motion. Aurelius raised a dark eyebrow and looked up, running his hand across his nose.

"I think that there is someone here to see you, *borde,*" the thief said.

"Most people would say 'hello', Caiside." Aurelius leaned back in his seat. "And yes, I am well, thank you. Who wants to see me?"

Caiside gestured towards the door. "Someone fancy, from the palace," he said, "I told them to wait outside."

"From the palace?" Aurelius straightened, wrapping his hand around the handle of his knife. "Did they give you a name?"

"No," the thief said, "but they are..." he paused, as if he could not figure out a tactful way to say what he was thinking. "*Like you,*" he finally managed. "Not *exactly* like you, but they are briney."

"*Briney.*" Aurelius shook his head. "That one is new." He squeezed his hand a little tighter around the knife. "Nothing good comes from the palace, especially not where the queen's kept pups are involved."

Caiside nodded his agreement. "If you invite them in, I can help you with the dismantling."

"I can handle it," Aurelius dismissed the offer, "are you certain they were alone?"

"As far as I could see," Caiside said. "Not a palace guard in sight. So, they are either desperate—or very naïve. Too much perfume in their head or something."

"Perhaps." Aurelius stroked his chin, running his thumb along the waxed hairs of his patterned beard. "If someone from the palace is carrying my name in their mouth, I want to know why. You can bring them in, but make sure that everyone stays alert."

Caiside nodded and stood, dragging his tankard with him as he went back to the door. Aurelius steeled himself, touching the leather sheathe strapped to his leg to reassure himself that his dagger was still within reach. The brass pin that kept his long black hair from tumbling into his eyes was a good nine inches long and thick enough to do significant damage in the right spot. He had taken out more than a few eyes that way.

Moments later, Caiside reappeared. The tall, graceful naiad by his side looked out of place in the cramped, dirty space. Although, they were not dressed as Aurelius might have expected. They wore a long black velvet robe that looked almost like a dressing gown. It had a high purple collar embroidered with gold, with matching satin cuffs that wrapped around their wrists and allowed the sleeves to billow behind. The sleeves were slit to show more flashes of purple satin, the wide streaks of color and ample piles of fabric serving to obscure as much blue-grey skin as possible. Their hair, bright orange with streaks of red, tumbled free around their shoulders—unusual, from what Aurelius understood. Most aristocrats wore their hair braided or snared in nets. They peered at him from behind round, gold-rimmed spectacles that rested on the end of their sharp nose, with a delicate gold chain swinging from either side to keep them in place.

They were the prettiest creature that Aurelius had seen in a long, long time. He adjusted himself in his seat accordingly and flicked a glance at Caiside.

"I think I can handle myself," he said by way of dismissal. Caiside looked unhappy, but he was not one to buck authority in front of a guest. He walked back to where the rest of the thieves sat, and they all turned their heads to watch.

If the palace pet was perturbed, they did not show it. They kept their hands clasped in front of them. There was a significant lack of jewelry on their person, which meant that they were not *entirely* naïve.

Aurelius gestured at the chair across from him. "Have a seat," he said.

The palace pet said nothing as they gathered the skirt of their robe in their hands and sat down.

"You are from the palace, I hear," Aurelius prompted. "If you are here on business, I need to know. If this is something else, it is only fair to warn you that every man in this tavern is mine—and not one of them will protest seeing your limbs thrown into the river."

The palace naiad's mouth quirked.

"Charming," they said. "You certainly have a way about you."

Aurelius leaned forward and set his arm against the table, unamused.

Those blue eyes followed every movement, quick and calculating.

"My name is Jules," they said. "And yes, I have come from the palace. It is unofficial business—as I am certain you might have guessed."

"Might have," Aurelius said.

"Are you Aurelius?" Jules asked. "Or is there another winged brute with a scarred lip and a nasty disposition that I should ask for?"

Aurelius laughed, more out of surprise than anything, and rolled his shoulders in response. The mention of his wings reminded him that they were there and made them itch. He wore them bound so often, these days, that it was easy to forget they existed—until the skin underneath the tight leather straps started to sweat.

"I am the only one, I am afraid," he said.

"Well." Those blue eyes sized him up again. "So, you are the harpy." They seemed to allow themselves a moment, the words skimming past their lips with an awed breath. After the moment passed, they collected themselves and tucked a strand of hair behind their pointed ear. "I came because I have need of information. I am willing to pay for it, of course."

"Of course," Aurelius allowed. "But how much?"

"It depends on what your information is worth." Jules adjusted their spectacles. "Who distributes the Glow down this way? I need a name."

"A name is worth a great deal," Aurelius said, furrowing his brow. "I thought the palace had their own private channels—you do not need the stuff from down here. It is cut with so much lye it will make your pretty head spin clean off your shoulders."

Jules wrinkled their nose. "It is not for personal fulfillment," they said. "And the *why* is certainly not your business to know—especially when *I* know that is not you."

"It could be," Aurelius challenged.

"Yet, it is not," Jules said. They reached into their robes and pulled out a heavy leather purse. They held it up by its strings, allowing it to dangle for a moment before dropping it to the table. It landed with a weighted *thud*.

"How do you know?" Aurelius did not reach out for the purse. He watched as Jules worked it open.

"You are a mercenary, not a drug-runner. You kill for gold, and you may use but you do not sell. They are two separate trades that rarely cross into one another." They took out three gold queen's head staters and set them, crown-side-up, on the table. "It is not worth lying to me."

Aurelius considered the coins, tilting his head to one side and running his fingertips over his beard. "Seems like not much of a risk, either way," he said, finally. "I could lie and take your coin. I could kill you, and still take it. Unless you can give me a few very good reasons to not do the latter, I feel you may be in a little over your head, sweeting."

Jules straightened their shoulders, bristling visibly. "Do you not ascribe to the rules of camaraderie? Peace between our own?"

"Why would I?" Aurelius asked. "Did you come here thinking that, because we are somewhat kindred, I would bend the rules for you? I suppose that makes it a bit clearer as to why you felt so bold. Let me tell you," he said and leaned in a little closer, "no one walks through the doors of my tavern, with palace gold and palace airs, pushing their nose into business that is not their own—and walks back out again. I guard my name and my face very closely."

He watched their face for signs of fear. He noticed how their lips pressed together and their eyes widened just a touch. They reached up to fuss with their spectacles again, and he could see the wheels turning.

"And, so," Jules finally said, "there is nothing to be done?"

Aurelius drummed his fingers on the surface of the table, pondering. It had been so long since anyone had come to this place asking for him directly. Word was always carried by messengers or by coins left with a name inside of a wooden post. From what he knew of the queen, she would not turn herself inside out if one of her pets went missing.

"Well," he said, "you could be initiated, I suppose."

Jules blinked.

"Pardon me?" they asked.

"If you swear yourself in as one of us," Aurelius smiled, unable to help his own amusement, and shrugged. "If your loyalty is to the troupe, then having you in the palace would be—like having a spy of my own, right under the queen's nose. I like that, actually, the more I consider it."

"I see." Jules pulled in a deep breath. "And you just allow anyone to join your numbers, do you? What are my qualifications, aside from my insistence on being allowed to live?"

"Can you read?" Aurelius asked.

"Of course." Jules sounded offended.

"There you have it. No one else here can," Aurelius spread his hands. "Aside from myself."

"Ah." Jules paused for a moment, as if they were weighing all their options before they resigned. "What is required of me?"

"Most have to prove themselves," Aurelius said. "Caiside spent three months trying before we finally let him swear the oath."

"I regret to inform you," Jules said a bit tightly, "that I do not have that kind of time."

"Of course not," Aurelius said. "There is another way, although it is slightly more unorthodox. And you seem…" He looked Jules up and down. "…highly resistant to the unorthodox."

"Try me." Jules folded their hands on the table.

Aurelius' smile widened.

"There are always exceptions," he said, "for those who marry in."

Silence would have dropped like a stone between them had it not been filled by the snickering of every thief at the table behind them. A coral flush swept over Jules' cheeks until their entire face was nearly the same shade of purple as their collar.

"Oh," Jules said, clearing their throat, "so, I am to choose from one of the illustrious bachelors sitting behind me?"

"You certainly could," Aurelius said. "Parsifal just got married last week, though, so you would have to ask his wife. Everyone else, to my knowledge, is free of attachment."

"And it does not bother you in any way that marriage between two people *or* creatures of the same sex is punishable by—need I go down the list of possibilities?"

"Oh, of course," Aurelius said dryly, "I have expressly chosen to break only a *few* laws. I abide by the rest as well as any other citizen."

Jules swallowed, plucking anxiously at a loose thread on their sleeve.

"And you?" they asked, raising their blue eyes once again. "Have you ever been married?"

"No," Aurelius said, "not once."

"Well," Jules scoffed under their breath, "no surprise, there." They rested their hands on the desk once again, unable to keep them still. "What expectations are attached to such marriage arrangements, aside from a complete willingness to chain oneself to a sinking boulder?"

"You act as though I have ever been caught," Aurelius said, "I never have."

"You are running a gamble with me," Jules retaliated, "as much as I am with you."

"If you betray us to the queen, after swearing an oath, there will not be enough pieces of you left to put back together for a funeral." Aurelius warned.

"It is not the queen you should worry about," Jules said, "I count the Admiral Blood as my friend."

"I heard that he is leaving," Aurelius probed as he met their gaze, "something about a mutiny."

"Sounds like an awful lot of hearsay." Jules' eyes did not waver. "Is it something you will stake your life on?"

Tension simmered in the air between them. Aurelius' heart was racing, although not from fear.

"Have you ever bedded a harpy?" he finally asked.

Jules threw their hands into the air and rolled their eyes.

"No!" they protested, completely flustered. "Nor will I!"

"That is a shame," Aurelius laughed, "it is one of the only benefits I can offer."

"I think you are a cur," Jules hissed, although their face was still purple, "and you can march straight into the mouth of Balam."

"You seem bent on getting there first." Aurelius extended his hand. "Unless you take me up on my offer."

"A pox on your offer, indeed," Jules muttered, although they reached across the table and grasped his hand. "You have not even given me the information I came for."

"Bad luck to do business on a wedding day," Aurelius said, "there will be time enough for that tomorrow."

"Tomorrow?" Jules scoffed, "you expect me to come back?"

"Have you forgotten your husband already?" Aurelius feigned hurt. "Surely, time drives a cruel wedge between us."

Jules released his hand, placing their fingers against their temple instead. "You are giving me a headache," they said. "What else is there to this ceremony, this oath? This complete sham?"

"My," Aurelius said, "is this how you always treat your suitors?"

"I have never been courted," Jules said, "if anyone ever does, I will report back."

"I will be interested to know," Aurelius said, "perhaps by then I can give them some advice." He gestured to the troupe. "Caiside," he called the thief back, "bring over a pitcher. A clay one."

Caiside did as he was told. He picked up a pitcher from the thieves' table, drank the last of what was inside, and then brought it over to where the naiads were sitting. Aurelius motioned for Jules to move back.

"You might want to pull your chair over," he said. "We need to break the pitcher."

"What for?" Jules asked.

"It is tradition," Caiside said. He held the pitcher up between them. "We break the pitcher to determine the length of your marriage contract."

"Oh." Jules rolled their eyes again. "I should have drawn that conclusion myself."

"From this day," Caiside said, "you will be bound together in marriage. And it will last for a period of..." he hefted the pitcher and threw it against the ground. It broke into four pieces, and he paused to count them. "...Four years," he announced to the room. "After that, you may go your separate ways in peace."

"Four years." Jules pinched the bridge of their nose. "May the Voyager help me."

"It is not a bad trade, if you were to ask me," Aurelius said. "Four years of loyalty, in exchange for the rest of your life? May they pass peaceably."

"I somehow doubt that they will," Jules said, "but I appreciate the sentiment, all the same."

"Here." From his coat, Aurelius pulled a small bottle. He pulled the tight cork and extended it across the table for Jules to inspect. "Brandy," he said. "Have a drink with me."

Jules inspected the contents of the bottle, tipping it to see if there was any oil shining on the surface and running their finger over the mouth for any traces of powder. Once they determined that it was likely not poisoned, they placed it against their lips and took a hesitant sip. They waited just a moment and then looked at Aurelius, knocking back a bigger mouthful before passing back the bottle.

"To marriage," Aurelius said, and took a drink.

"Mm." Jules swallowed. "To business." They held their hand over their mouth. "What sort of food do they serve here?"

"Nothing that you would want to eat," Aurelius told them. "The King's Head has something better. Lamb stew, I think, on the right day."

"Well." Jules swept up their purse, although they left the three gold staters on the table. "I believe that your first act as a married man will be to take me there."

Aurelius laughed. "All right." He stood. "if you can bear to be seen with me."

"If I can bear to smell you, I can bear to be seen with you," Jules said. "Do not mistake me, sir, I have a reputation as well—although outside the castle, and I suspect for you outside of this tavern, our faces blend together for those who do not know better."

Aurelius' smile faded a bit. "That much is true," he said, "to be so markedly different that we become invisible—it can, at times, work in our favor as much as it works against us."

"Indeed." Jules inclined their chin and gestured, "after you."

---·---

JOURNAL ENTRY

NOTES ON HESTER PRIMUS

T HERE IS NOTHING I can say about Hester Primus
that would be flattering.

He is hated, and he deserves every bit of it. He was
the first to arrive—the first naiad ever captured by the
queen. That, I suppose, would be enough to make him a
bastard—but I believe that there was blackness in his heart
before she ever sought to corrupt it.

When Hester was captured, the queen had him tortured
on the beach. I know that she ordered his brineskin to
be cut away. That is its own wretched agony that I cannot comprehend enduring. Our brineskins were created
to be removed, *however, to be relinquished willingly.* Hester
still bears the scars. The soldiers used knives with ragged
edges, and the wounds they left behind—even now, so
many years later—look like healed burns.

Once she took his brineskin, she burned it. He was not
even an hour on the shore. He was forced to shift into
something appearing more human or die there, on the
sand. The queen learned a great deal about naiads that
day. She was unhappy with him that he could not assume a

color different than the one he was born with—that dusky pale blue. She learned that we stick out, even on land—yet realized just as quickly that she could use even that to her advantage. She learned that burning the brineskin meant that she had lost a great deal of her leverage, but she made up for it—she had him by the throat from the very start.

Of course, Hester beds the queen. That is known and accepted. It is her way of maintaining control, and I believe that she finds some perverse satisfaction in exercising her power over him, knowing how he hates her.

And despite his hatred, he serves her well. Hester is responsible for the increased capture and slaughter of our numbers. The queen had a dozen uses for naiad bodies before, and he has since supplied her with a hundred more. I fear it will only get worse. I am convinced that the only thing Hester hates more than the queen is himself, and it is his own self-loathing that propels him to commit such atrocities against our kin.

He is a sorcerer, although sources vary on what kind. I believe he is a necromancer. I have never asked him about his magic, nor have I ever seen it practiced—save for the odd trick at court that the queen will demand as a display for her guests. He is the Court High Sorcerer, and she has named him one of her ambassadors. What he could have to say to a foreign dignitary, I have no idea, but I also have no doubt that it would plunge us into a long-awaited war. Perhaps then, as pique irony, his actions would be what sets the rest of us free.

Another detail that I must not neglect is that Hester does not have a nose. Cahal was the one who took it. He sliced it clean off, and the queen did not care to discipline him. I wish, with all my heart, that I knew the particulars of that story. All I can say is that it resulted in Hester wearing a false gold nose, and it left him with a scar—one that cuts down his eye and across his face. There are other parts of him missing—a few fingers, namely, which he disguises with stuffed gloves. He bears down on his cane heavier than I do with my own, and I am not sure of why—except I believe that his bones are fragile. All of him is fragile. In the warmest weather, he would still wear velvet and furs. He complains that the cold makes him ache. I believe that it makes him incontinent.

I have mentioned before that Jules hates Hester, and I hope that this gives some insight as to why. Jules does not hate without cause. I, myself, long for the day when Hester can be formally cast from the Society. Until then, we must all bear the lesser of two evils. We do not want, or need, his ire and retribution.

Hester

Hester

The Iniquitous Judge

THE QUEEN'S BEDCHAMBER WAS suffused with a heavy cloud of incense; an opulent room that would have made a pantheon of gods feel undeserving of its splendor. Her raised bed played the role of an altar, covered in rich green silk and cloth-of-gold, sheltered by jacquard curtains and anchored by an intricately carved redwood frame that had been passed down the family line with the same linear diligence as the crown itself. The incense was all that Hester could smell, although his senses were already dampened by his lack of a nose. It covered up everything, leaving his tongue to decipher the rest—such as the bitter taste of alcohol on her perfumed breasts, or the salt on her warm thighs.

His false gold nose was covered in her grease. He wiped it clean with a handkerchief and tightened the leather lace that held it fixed underneath his chin.

He was waiting for her dismissal. His mind had already started sifting through a hundred tasks that required his attention the moment he was able to leave.

The queen, for her part, must have been feeling indulgent. She sat propped up against her headboard, enthroned on the rumpled bedcovers with her poppy-red hair cascading over her bone-white shoulders, a disrupted curtain of silk. She studied him intently with her chin tilted down, gazing up at him with eyes as green as Avralaenian hillocks.

The silence between them was uncomfortable, like sitting on a boar-bristle brush.

"By your leave, your majesty." Hester tried not to sound impatient. She raised an eyebrow at him as disapproval twisted her full pink mouth.

"You are eager to depart this evening," she sounded displeased.

"There is a fresh catch to be broken down," Hester said, sliding one hand over the other and wishing for his gloves. "And I thought you would have been satisfied."

"You think highly of yourself, then." 'the queen spread her arms across the pillows piled up behind her and crossed her legs. "I have had more stimulating pony rides."

"Cut out my tongue then, if it does not serve you," he scoffed. Hester stood; he was still mostly dressed, but the rest of his clothes had been thrown over the back of a nearby chair where the fireplace had kept them warm. He sought out his gloves, first, slipping them on so that the stuffed fingertips could conceal the two that were missing on his left hand.

"How many pieces of you will I have taken, then?" she asked idly. "You will start to miss them."

"There is little of this flesh for me to miss. I hardly feel it." It was the sorry repercussion of having his brineskin ripped away. Before her majesty realized that it was better to have them handed over (or stolen from wherever they were poorly stowed away), she had skinned him like a seal and forced him to take on a new form for the sake of staying alive. He had been her first, so her work was sloppy. The twisted, shiny scars on his back and his chest served as a constant reminder, wrinkled like burns.

"You still lie to me," she said. "You screamed loudly enough when Admiral Ivers took off your nose."

He flicked his tongue over his sharp teeth, his lips bulging in distaste. "I do not recall."

"His hilt bounced off the ridge of your eye. He cracked the bone. You do not recall?" She twisted a crimson lock around her fine index finger. "You bear his scars."

"Scars do not remember pain, only faces." Hester finished buttoning his vest and pulled on his long black velvet frock coat. The cuffs flared in a foreign style and turned upward to show off the blue and silver brocade lining. As many layers as he wore, he could not shake the dense cold that permeated his frail body. "Ivers—there is a face that cannot be forgotten."

"You are one to make such a claim," the queen said. Hester shrugged his shoulders and picked up his dark mink stole. It fastened with a thin silver chain across his chest—perhaps his favorite layer, because it was the softest to the touch and provided the most heat.

"By your leave," he said again. She swept her hand through the air in irate dismissal.

"I will see your reports on my desk tomorrow morning," she said. "You may leave out the details of your methods, this time, I am only interested in the results."

"There is nothing erroneous in my reports," Hester hissed and raised his chin. "The results are in the method."

"That may very well be, and yet I am not interested. Save your musings and your observations for your private journals, Hester, and give me only what I need."

He bowed his head, hating her.

Hester made his way to the door and grabbed his cane from where it rested against the wall. He gripped the brass head so fiercely that, had the metal been of any lesser quality, his fingers would have left an indent.

T HE LOWEST LEVELS OF the palace prison smelled brackish like seawater. The last few stairs leading down into a circular stone chamber were wet and crumbling, to the point where Hester did not trust them with the full of his weight. A guard held out his hand for the sorcerer, and Hester clutched it for support as he made his descent.

His new prisoner's screeching was already grating on his nerves. Nothing could scream quite like a landed naiad whose lungs were burning from the dry surface air.

"How many hours has it been?" he asked above the ear-splitting sound. The guard across from him had given up on speaking altogether and signed in shroudcant.

'Two hours', the guard signed. Hester nodded his acknowledgement and walked over to the cell, grinding the tip of his cane against the stone and crossing his hands over the head so that he could lean forward and peer through the bars.

The naiad was small for its kind, and already it appeared mostly human. In the water, they were more creatures than anything – but when shedding their brineskin, they looked like the things of a sailor's tavern songs. This one had a bright yellow tail with ragged blue fins as wide as sails. The tail itself filled up most of the cell—but when it was shed completely, it would be thinner than a pressed reed and softer than silk. It would be easy to collect, then.

His only gripe was that there was no knowing how long it could take. It could be hours; it could be a day. It was entirely dependent upon how long the creature was willing to ration its breath before submitting to the inevitable.

There had been only one instance where the naiad had been too young, and once the brineskin fell off there was nothing below the waist but bone and jellied organs.

Hester took a step back and sought out his chair. A guard brought it forward for him and he sat down carefully, keeping his eyes on the naiad as it twisted and thrashed in its enclosure. Its great yellow tail hit the iron bars with such force that they rattled, and the guards around him could not keep their nervous expressions down.

"Keep yourselves at ease," he said. "What is it going to do, if it escapes?"

"Eat us," one of them muttered. Hester sneered.

"That thing is pure *hváll*," he said. "They are as gentle as they are massive. You are in no danger unless you are made out of kelp."

"It tore a chunk off Brutus, getting it here," another one of the guards said. "Almost capsized the boat before we could give it opium."

"Which seems to be wearing off." Hester never moved his gaze away from the cell. "I will start taking my notes now and review what her majesty wants from this one." Now that he was sitting, he no longer had need of his cane. He handed it off in exchange for his journal, the vellum pages of which were weighed down heavily by ink and rippled from use. He turned to where a broad red ribbon had been laid between the pages and ran his finger down an ordered list of her majesty's requests. "Perfume," he said, "so we will take the bladder. Fat for a new shipment of oil. If we are taking all of that, then..." He gestured for his pen, and a guard knelt down beside him, holding the quill and ink. Hester accepted the quill without a word, dipping it in the inkwell before scratching out a few more notes. "We will take the hide, and I want the bones boiled until they are clean. Check the hair – if it is good quality enough to be sold, cut it neatly and bind it with ribbon. Do you know," he sidetracked his own words, "they say our hair makes the softest lace."

The guards did not seem to know what to say to that, and he did not expect them to reply. He kept writing.

"Her majesty's physician thinks he can make something of the organs, so I will allow him those, since they are typically thrown out. He will be disappointed that we have no poison glands to give him, but this is the wrong sort. The flesh..."

"...Your excellency," one of the guards hesitated before he spoke, "if I may interject that...the last time we ground up what was leftover, it made the queen's hounds sick. There are some farmers who claim it had the same effect on their pigs."

"And I am sure it would affect you the same way," Hester clipped. "I will mark that down. If the pigs cannot eat it, then someone will have to. Perhaps the queen's guard."

The guard fell silent and for a moment, the only sound was the scratching of the sorcerer's quill. Hester looked up as soon as he finished, dropping the quill back into the inkwell and handing his journal over to the guard beside him.

"It looks as though we are ready to proceed." He wished, not for the first time, that his chair had wheels to move on its own. If the queen would have allowed it, he would not hesitate to have one made. Standing and sitting, sitting and then standing, was almost too laborious a task.

The guards understood their cue. Two of them stepped over to the cell and unlocked it, one more standing at the ready with a cudgel in case the prisoner became out-of-hand. The naiad's vivid brineskin had shriveled and dulled, as empty as a shed snakeskin. One of the guards pinched it up and began gathering it in his hands, his face twisted visibly in disgust at handling the supple, flabby hide. Once the cell had been cleared, the second guard stepped in to gather up the prisoner. The naiad was taller than he was, but their legs were still weak. Their knees wobbled and their head lolled, although they were clearly still conscious. Their semi-lucid state was betrayed by a harrowing light from their bright orange eyes.

Hester smiled, showing all his vicious teeth.

His favorite part of processing a catch came down to one rousing decision. Did he inform them of their fate, or did he tell them nothing at all, and watch the terror and dawning horror break in waves across their confused face? He had retained enough Brebble to convey the dire words. The naiad continued to stare at him with eyes like drowned lanterns on the sides of a sinking ship.

He did not look away from them, even as he spoke to the guards. "Begin your work," he said. "I will observe."

There was nothing on the naiad's face to indicate that they understood him. However, when the guards wheeled the table around, their defiant expression shifted into something a little more uncertain. The naiad let out another wretched, keening wail as they were lifted off the ground and thrown down onto the table. Hester inhaled sharply, soaking it in as if he could suck the sound from the air through his teeth and use it to imbue his rotted heart with new life.

Heavy chains rattled as they were pulled from their hooks on the side of the table's base. One of the guards splayed his hand across the naiad's cheek as he held their head down in place, which in turn kept it facing the seated sorcerer. The sheer terror and lack of understanding that resulted in a bewitching junction of the naiad's misting eyes and their partially open, trembling mouth sent an inexorable quiver down to his groin.

It was joined, of course, by another rumble entirely, and he knew that he would not be able to stay long. The prison cold was seeping through his clothing and his back ached from the rigid posture it was forced to maintain. As much as he wanted to stay, he would have to rely on the prison reports.

Hester closed his eyes. He wanted to hold on for as long as possible to soak in every whimper and yelp. He wanted to be present for when the naiad started to beg. That was what he desired the most, truly. Even in coarse, babbling Brebble—pleas for mercy were as gratifying as a meal. Hester rarely desired food. He sought out, instead, those rare moments of genuine terror that made his eyes glaze over and put warmth in his chest that spread faster, and hotter, than any liquor.

He dug his nails into the sides of his knee. His gloves blunted their pointed tips, a small mercy for his ruined joints. His breath stuck in his throat and for a moment, his vision swam. The naiad's face blurred except for the focal point of their shiny, quivering lips—soft shell pink and torn apart by their own teeth. All that mattered were the sounds. How akin they were to ecstasy, at their base, and yet so far removed from the delicate intimacy of a bedroom.

The pain in his stomach was becoming too much to bear. Hester swallowed and held out his hand, gesturing for one of the soldiers to come over to his side.

"Hand me my cane," he hissed when they obeyed. His mouth felt dry, and yet, the corners of his mouth were damp.

The guard scrambled to pass him his cane and Hester gripped the head like a lifeline. He pulled himself to his feet and took one long, last look at the naiad spread out on the table like a sacrifice. The dissection had not even begun, and every trace of pride and defiance had already been wiped from their face.

That, at least, was satisfaction enough. They opened their mouth as if to speak, and he waited with baited breath.

The sound that passed through their lips was a faint one. Brebble was a language made to pass through the darkest depths of the water, high and piercing like a whale's song, clacking and chattering like a dolphin. It could be soft, or it could be fast and merry. Now, for him, it was mournful, and he understood enough of it to know it was a cry for pity.

He leaned forward over his cane, despite his own pain, and crooned back in the language of his birth. *"It will be over soon."* Something to that effect, although it was not meant to be soothing – it was simply a promise.

The horror that seized the naiad's face was enough for him. Hester turned away and carried that satisfaction with him all the way to the top of the stairs—feeling somewhat sated, it had not all been for waste.

IN THE SANCTUARY OF his bedchamber, a hot bath was Hester's only solace. His position within the court bestowed him with luxurious accommodations on the East wing of the castle, not inaccessible to the queen but well-away from most other courtiers he wished to avoid. The suite was smaller than most, although it had been constructed that way to accommodate a private bath. Only three other compartments boasted their own, and those were the king's chamber, the queen's chamber, and the set of rooms belonging to Lord Marcellus Andronicus.

The bathtub itself was twice the size it needed to be. He had ordered one to be crafted out of copper on the philosophy that it soothed his joints. It could have accommodated another body or two, but no one other than a single trusted servant had ever been allowed that far into his sanctum.

After all, he was hated enough. He did not need it spread throughout the castle that Lord Hester Primus, High Court Sorcerer to the queen, fouled his bath water—even if it was only on occasion. There had been a few instances where he had not been able, or willing, to pull himself out when the pain overtook his body and he was weary from having been bludgeoned by it.

The servant who brought his hot water was without a tongue, which also aided in his immaculate discretion.

The pain in Hester's back was already fading with the addition of hot water and the relief of having reached his chamber pot. His worn, frail body sank into the water –

overwhelmed by fragrant oils drawn from soaked peppermint leaves and dried mountain rosebuds.

He closed his eyes and thought of the naiad's final words—those woeful, burbling sounds. The soft clicks of its tongue. The imploring gaze. He gripped the sides of the bath and took another deep breath. Peppermint filled his lungs and cleared his torn nasal passages, while the temporal release from his pain allowed the deep quiver in his chest to spread warmth down between his legs. A comfortable arousal.

Hester opened his eyes when he heard nails drumming against the rim of the tub. His servant, whose name might have been Fintan, regarded him with uncanny orange eyes.

Fintan signed to him in shroudcant, asking if he required anything more.

Hester shook his head and flicked his hand in dismissal. "Go," he said. "I will call for you when I have need."

Fintan bowed and backed away, obedient without complaint. Hester watched him retreat, and then dove his hands back underneath the water to savor what was left of his memory.

A Letter to Jules

In Regard to Hester

T EXT TAKEN FROM A *half-burned note discovered in the ashes of the royal library fireplace.*

My love,

Your carefully culminated hatred for Hester Primus, and all he stands for, may finally have its time to serve us. You will see, enclosed, some reports taken from his desk that I knew would find their way to you eventually, but I took it upon myself to expedite their journey.

Come up to the tower and lend me your thoughts. We have much to discuss.

Yours,
S.

Journal Entry

Regarding the Queen's Huntsman

THE QUEEN'S HUNTSMAN IS Fabian Wruck. She gifted him both names, with the latter translating loosely to mean 'cantankerous'. Which, I find, turned out to be very well-suited.

Fabian was the last to arrive, at least of all who are in the palace now. He was lost to us as soon as he walked through the doors, falling immediately into the arms of Hester Primus. Fabian and Hester are of the same brood, which is the only explanation I can conjure for why they get along so well. And it is here that I use 'get along' for its loosest possible interpretation.

They share a bed and a gift for hating, and beyond that, there are times when I do not believe that they even like each other. Yet, it is not my position to speculate too closely on the particulars. Hester seems to gravitate towards anyone who is bent on humiliating him, or who treats him with the proper amount of revulsion that his outward appearance demands. I have found Fabian to be incredibly possessive of Hester in a way that is puzzling, mostly because I was not aware that he was being faced with any competition.

Returning to Fabian's role, the Huntsman. It reads better than 'assassin' on paper, yet that is truly what he is. He is loyal to the Queen, and to Hester—and thus, he cannot be trusted. He is a member of our fold by the same formalities and principles with which we allowed Hester to take part.

I find Fabian to be a deeply complex individual, though not one that I would dedicate my life to studying. He is distant and taciturn in an observational way, as opposed to a melancholy one. He is direct, and he has a temper, although I have yet to see it truly get away from him. I believe that his heart is not in his work. He seems content amongst humans and is easy to overlook—despite his unusual coloration and markings, his ash-grey skin and the wide yellow stripe that runs down the center of his face. Perhaps, under different circumstances, Fabian would follow a far simpler calling.

Unfortunately, I will never know for certain.

Fabian

Fabian

The Unyielding Huntsman

I T WAS A PITIFUL thing to be jealous over, yet Fabian could not bring himself to care. He was far more interested in the sound of squelching mud and popping cartilage that came as he drove his heel against the back of the aristocrat's neck. Court High Aristocracy or not, Her Majesty would only tolerate so much from her more derelict subjects. And Fabian was willing to lower her threshold to the standard of his own in the face of a personal slight. He could engender an execution if he wanted to, and he was not certain that the perfume-soaked fop writhing under his boot understood that.

He applied a little more pressure to his heel and leaned over, resting his elbow on his knee and lowering his chin. A few wild tendrils of white hair sprang free from their tether and fell into his face as he addressed the vagrant beneath him.

"Lord Darcey," he said, "it is my understanding that you seem to have lost track of where your seat is at Her Majesty's table."

The nobleman sputtered, gargling mud as his hands clawed at the dark, soaked earth. Above their heads, a thick veil of clouds broke apart just enough to allow some moonlight to shine through. Fabian waited for the span of another heartbeat before he pulled back and graciously allowed his prisoner some room to move.

Lord Darcey dragged himself up to his knees. His painted face was coated with mud, and when he opened his mouth, he pushed out a clump of the stuff with his tongue. The aristocrat looked mortified as he spat out even more, clutching his stomach as if the rest was going to come up on a stream of bile. His pastel-pink coat was ruined, and a spill of expensive lace hung in tatters around his throat. He looked like he had been run over by a carriage.

He reached up to rub the back of his neck, throwing a cutting green glare at the huntsman's face as he snarled through the grit in his teeth. "I know my place, *múrauch,*" he spat out the slur with some more mud. "Although you seem to be less aware of your own."

Fabian's lips tightened into something that was not quite a smile. "*Múrauch?* You cannot use such filthy language against brinefolk while also getting on your knees for Lord Hester Primus. Or do you swallow your pride when you push his cock down your throat? I do not think he would take kindly to that revelation."

Lord Darcey sneered, an expression that did not serve its intended purpose of covering up his fear. "Lord Hester? There is nothing of mine I would risk to put my tongue against that shit-smeared shortsword."

"Oh?" Fabian lowered his voice, "so you were speaking on matters of the Chamber, his lordship and yourself?"

"We were discussing the trade embargo being enforced against the North..." Lord Darcey's words were cut off as Fabian brought a hand down against the back of his head. He wore a plate of silver across the back of his knuckles, strung around his fingers with individual rings. The huntsman rolled his eyes upward as Darcey went down and placed his boot against the aristocrat's back once again.

"His lordship has never given a shit about Graueyette, or the trade embargos against it, or you." Fabian's hand dropped down to the soft dagger sheath hanging from his belt. "I will give you one more opportunity to tell me the truth. And you may consider that a mercy."

Lord Darcey clutched at the back of his head and his fingers came back bloody. It all looked black in the moonlight, but it was still wet, and the pale light made it glisten. His hand trembled visibly, and his larynx convulsed as if he could not quite force himself to swallow.

"You are betrayed by your own attachment," Darcey sputtered. "Whatever deposition you make against me will not bear comparison with the evidence of your brutality, coupled with what I know of you and your relationship with the Lord High Sorcerer. The Queen will see you hanged." Even as he ranted, his words were slurring.

Fabian slipped the dagger free of its sheath and slid his foot away from the nobleman's back, making sure to drag his sole and smear more mud onto the fabric.

"I will have the stronger case," Fabian said. "The queen almost never questions my reasoning for cutting out a tongue."

Before the aristocrat could process his words, Fabian grabbed him by the face. He dug his fingers onto Darcey's stunned cheeks, smearing white paint all over his worn leather gloves. Fabian scrunched his brow in displeasure, but it was not enough to distract him from his work. He squeezed the aristocrat's face until Darcey's tongue popped out, and he pinched the tip, pulling it free until there was over two inches exposed. Fabian's blade cut cleanly through, as if the red organ was softer than cheese. More blood spouted from the stump and he pushed it back into Darcey's mouth, holding his gloved hand down to seal the entrance. He did not speak for those first few moments, content to watch the artistocrat's face turn purple and listen to him choke on his own blood until it started spewing from his nose.

"Let that be a lesson to you, then," Fabian's voice, when he spoke again, was almost a whisper. "You may sit across from Lord Hester in chamber, but I stand behind him. And the next time you touch what belongs to me, you will lose more than just a tongue." He released his hold on the unfortunate lord, straightening himself up enough to walk away. He tread on Darcey's hand as he departed, almost smiling at the pained winced that was followed by a wretched sob.

THE LAMP OIL WAS burning low, but the dimming light was not enough to deter Hester from finishing out his paperwork. He sat hunched over his desk, only not swathed in his usual mass of furs because of his close proximity to the fire. Fabian watched him from the cold shadows, his arms crossed so tightly over his chest that they started to tingle.

Hester did not raise his head when he spoke. "Is there something that I can do for you?"

Fabian stepped into the light. He had been clenching Darcey's tongue in his hand, so it was still warm—but also pale and bloody, covered in grime and scrunched by his fist. It looked like an undercooked piece of fish or pheasant, and not at all like something that had been once attached to a person. He slammed it down on the desk and pulled his hand away, leaving it to soak the corner of Hester's parchment.

The sorcerer looked over and made a vague sound of disgust.

"What is that?" Hester asked, picking it up and rubbing it between his fingers.

"You should recognize it," Fabian said shortly, "it is Lord Darcey's tongue."

"Oh." Hester set the tongue back down. "He did not have much use for it, anyway."

"He put it to hard work very recently, so I hear." Fabian set both hands on Hester's desk and leaned over until he was looming over his lover. "Or are you going to lie to me, as well?"

Hester finally looked up. His cold, silver eyes betrayed nothing beyond a mild irritation, what looked like milk in the process of curdling. "I said *much* use." He swiped his tongue over his teeth. "He is better off without it in both chambers."

Fabian's lip curled. "There is still enough of your face left that I could ruin it," he said. "Do not make me carve out your few redeeming features just because you cannot refrain from dribbling your seed down some dandy's throat."

Hester picked up the piece of tongue once again and held it between them, not pulling his eyes away from the naiad in front of him. "What's got your dander up, Fabian? Have you not eaten?" He pressed the bit of organ against Fabian's pressed mouth. Fabian growled, slightly baring his teeth.

"Do not patronize me," he said.

"You are so jealous of a wet little *human* aristocrat who means nothing to you otherwise." Hester pushed his fingers insistently against Fabian's mouth, forcing them between the huntsman's teeth and shoving the bit of tongue inside. It tasted like dirt, but Fabian snapped it up anyway. Rather than spit it out, he ground it between his teeth until it was two pieces and then swallowed. When he had finished, he grabbed hold of Hester's wrist, keeping the sorcerer's hand in his mouth while sucking on his fingers, rolling his tongue around them.

If that flustered or moved the sorcerer at all, there was no easy way to tell—unless one was looking closely, and noted the way Hester's scarred lips parted just enough to let a hitched breath eke out.

"And so," Hester continued with an edge around his words, "if you are quite through being fussy, perhaps I might turn your attention towards a more flagrant slight."

"What slight?" Fabian pulled Hester's hand away from his mouth but kept his hold, massaging the tight tendons across his lover's knuckles.

Hester used his free hand to tap the parchment in front of him. Fabian pinched the edge and pulled it up from the desk, holding it to the light. He recognized the square, uncomplicated handwriting and the practical shorthand penned by someone who could not be bothered for a more formal deposal, not even to honor the perception of respect between two Court High officials.

"Sopespian?" Fabian asked, reading on before his question could be answered. "He has expelled you from the Society?"

"He believes that he can." Hester sucked on his teeth. "Since it came to light that Her Majesty intends to expand our hunting territory into Dragolothian waters. I am not certain of how he came to possess this information—but I will start squeezing oil out of bladders before the week's end. Nothing a slick-tongued traitor cannot live without."

"If he is angry at Her Majesty, then why are you expelled?" Fabian set the letter back down.

"He has been turning himself inside-out for years trying to pull together a landslide vote to have me ousted," Hester said. "With Cahal Ivers gone, there is no one left to dig in their heels. Except for you. And that will not be good enough."

Fabian tightened his jaw and straightened his posture. "What do you want me to do?" he asked.

"What you are good for," Hester said. "Just an hour ago you took a man's tongue for some imagined infidelity. Will you not take another from someone who has dealt me a grievous insult?"

Fabian glanced down at the paper. Sopespian, though Fabian never liked him, had been the caretaker of them all. Hester had been the first to be taken by the queen, but Sopespian was the one who united them in spite of their differences. The astronomer was the only one capable of standing up against Cahal's temper, of bearing Hester's cruelty, and of soothing Jules' nerves. Bravery, or madness, whatever it was—it was enough to earn a grain of Fabian's respect. Only a grain—but enough that he was hesitant to inflict harm.

Bucking against Hester's will, however, was enough to get anyone killed. Fabian knew that better than most. And he was certain, as well, that the sorcerer would not hesitate to lash out at him if he failed to follow through on an order. His punishment would be cruel, although it was unlikely to be swift.

"Is the tongue all that you want?" Fabian asked, drawing his eyes back up to meet Hester's. The sorcerer raised his mutilated eyebrow.

"The tongue is all I will demand," Hester said, "the rest I will leave up to your discretion. I will be taking note, however, of what pieces you leave intact. Bear that in mind.

I do not think I will take kindly to the sight of him walking upright, after all he has done."

Fabian exhaled sharply and walked around the desk, covering his exasperation with his pacing. He was good at framing things as requests or suggestions when they were, in fact, neither. "When I come back," he said, "I am claiming my reward."

"You assume you will be rewarded for doing as you are told," Hester said. "You are the queen's huntsman, but I am your master. She does not care about your life, and I will pull rank to see it ruined."

Fabian rolled his eyes. "Pull rank with me," he said. "I will follow through with my threats about your face. You forget that I am the only naiad in this castle who has not taken my fair share of it."

"I do not forget," Hester said. "There is a reason that I allow you into my bed."

"And yet, you disparage me for coveting my place."

"I think you are too territorial for your own good," Hester said, "and you need to be reminded of your place."

"My place!" Fabian threw his hands into the air. He melted back into the shadows, where any words that Hester might have thrown after him were lost.

T HE ASTRONOMY TOWER WAS the highest point of the palace, although it did not boast much of a view.

Out one small window no wider than an archer's slit, there was a fairly unimpeded view of the ocean. By that, the white strip of beach was barely visible, and beyond the churning waves there was nothing—just a syrupy line of blue where the horizon and the water began to blur. The rickety, unsealed wooden floor groaned with the slightest additional pressure—already overburdened by haphazard stacks of books that looked like they had been hauled up from the castle library. In the center of the room was Sopespian's pride and joy, what was dearer to him than any child—a large brass telescope with its wide, dewy lens pointed upward at the glass dome ceiling. Above Fabian's head, through the impossibly clear glass, the stars looked close enough to grasp.

"Do I want to know why you are here?" Sopespian's voice, one that Fabian had always found to be a bit sneering and smug, floated across the room. There was not enough light to pick the astronomer out of the shadows, so Fabian stayed where he was with his hands resting loosely by his side.

"I think that you could speculate," Fabian reached into his pocket and pulled out a lump of rock embedded with some crystal points. "I brought an offering."

From nearer than he expected, the astronomer's hand snaked out of the darkness and plucked the rock from his palm. Sopespian's head tilted down to study the offering, his bright red curls tumbling around his face while the tip of his tongue dragged its way along his bottom lip. He wore a curious monocle strapped to his head—one which was actually three of different sizes, with the largest one near his eye and the smallest, no bigger than a thumbnail, resting close to his nose. He seemed content to ignore Fabian completely, hunched over his new treasure like a gloating dragon. He took a seat on top of a stool, keeping his shoulders and back bowed to make himself seem smaller. When he stood straight, he was taller than Fabian—taller than most in the court.

Fabian allowed him a few minutes of inquisitive examination before opening his mouth to break the silence. Sopespian cut him off before he could even draw in a new breath.

"So." Sopespian looked up at last. "Hester is upset?" The largest lens on his monocle made his orange right eye look enormous. Its normal-sized twin was half-obscured by a curl.

"An understatement." Fabian nodded. "I would say...perhaps, the largest understatement that you could make."

Sopespian snorted. "I anticipated as much." He turned the rock around in his busy fingers. "I should have expected that he would send you."

"He knows that I will do it," Fabian lowered his voice, "and that I know how. He wants your tongue."

Sopespian flicked his tongue over his lips again. "It is my tongue," he said a bit petulantly, "I am attached to it."

"It is not all he wants," Fabian warned.

"He wants an apology? He wants to be reinstated?" Sopespian guessed, flashing a smile. "He wants us to line up, fall to our knees one-by-one, and kiss his ring? Or..." He adjusted his tiered monocle. "He just wants me dead?"

"I think he will settle for all four," Fabian said.

"Ah." Sopespian slid off his stool, rolling the rock he was still holding around in his palm. "It is a terrible thing, to not get what one wants. I know that Hester never learned how to take it."

"Sopespian," Fabian tried to convey the direness of the astronomer's situation, "I will not leave here without a body."

Sopespian's eyes drifted up and down the huntsman's form and he ground the tip of his tongue between his sharp teeth. His gaze seemed unfocused, hazy, as if he were so far down the tunnel of his own thoughts that he was no longer connected to the present.

"Well," Sopespian finally said, "you will not leave here with mine, either." He turned to face the window and bounced the rock in his hand, a string of unspoken words rumbling in his throat. "Tell Hester that you could not find me."

"That will work," Fabian said dryly. "I am certain he will have no cause for doubt."

Sopespian shook his head. "How many days since Cahal left?"

Fabian did not know. "Three?" he guessed.

"Two. I wrote that letter to Hester within the same hour. And," Sopespian stroked his chin, "I had a servant deliver it to his desk. So, so, he has not laid eyes on me in nearly a week."

"Although *someone* has," Fabian argued. "Jules does not go a day without setting his eyes on you."

"Jules will never tell." Sopespian smiled again. "And Cahal and I had a falling out. You heard about that, did you not?"

"I saw the blood," Fabian said, "it is still in the stairwell. I stepped over it to make my way to you."

"Ran me clean through, and it hurt," Sopespian said, "but it missed every vital organ."

"Praise to the Voyager." Fabian folded his arms. "So, you are going to disappear, and everyone will think that Cahal killed you?"

"Is that not gruesome enough to satisfy you?"

Fabian bit the inside of his cheek. "Hester is smarter than that."

"Maybe," Sopespian said, "I will have to take your word for it. However, on the off-chance that he is not, I will be long-gone by the time he is able to send out a royal search party."

Fabian rubbed his palm against the end of his chin. "That is treason."

"Yes," Sopespian said, "and the queen will burn my brineskin. The Red Star Society will dissolve without my leadership, and that is just what Hester wants. If he cannot have my tongue, then the dismantling of my organization will have to do."

"I am taking your tongue," Fabian said.

"No," Sopespian countered, "you are not."

Fabian was starting to wish that he had led the conversation more aggressively, possibly with a knife. "They will hunt down Cahal, too," Fabian pointed out.

"I would not waste my worry on Cahal, or his safety," Sopespian said. "He will outlive us both." He brushed his fingers over the ridge of his telescope, his glib and vacant expression suddenly smothered by a touch of melancholy. "I will miss it," he said, although he did not make it clear what he was referring to. When he looked up, his bright orange eyes were dim. "I wish that I had studied you better," he said. "You are a cannibalistic sort, are you not? *Áaoll*, like Hester—you eat your own."

Something stuck in Fabian's throat and he could not swallow it down. "It is our nature," he managed at last. "I fear you judge him too harshly for it."

"No," Sopespian said, "I do not. I have watched Cahal break the hands of prisoners and I have watched Jules pour poison into the ears of sleeping aristocrats. I saw Ephraim slice open a man's larynx and I, myself, have cajoled Her Majesty for funding of experiments that would turn the gods' heads in revulsion. Of everyone here, I think you, Fabian—are perhaps the most conscience-plagued amongst us. What is Hester's sin, then? Can you bring yourself to speculate?"

"He is a cannibal." Fabian did not need to think about it. "He hunts his own."

"Hunts, tortures, murders—he cuts us up and distributes our body parts like wares." Sopespian nodded gravely. "He abets the queen, but they are just as vile as each other. The Society began so that we could protect one another. If Hester cannot see all he has done to relinquish his right to that protection, then he is a cancer, and he must be cut out." Sopespian sighed. "I took it upon myself to do it, so

I will pay the price. It will be on the rest of you to sustain it."

"Who? Jules? Myself?" Fabian watched the astronomer move.

"There will always be more," Sopespian said. He picked up a leather bag and plopped it down on top of his stool, picking up some nearby items and shoving them inside. "Especially if Hester gets his way."

Fabian knew that if he did not stop Sopespian, now, the astronomer would be gone—and he would have to explain himself to the Lord Sorcerer. He had hunted plenty on Hester's behalf, and on the queen's command—he did as he was told. He was dutiful. Loyal.

He watched Sopespian finish packing. He could not bring himself to move.

"I want it known," Fabian started to speak again, and Sopespian paused, "that I never thought much of you. Yet, what I did think...was venerable." He did not know how else to say it. Sopespian accepted his words, inclining his head and slipping up his monocle so that Fabian could meet his gaze unimpeded.

"I doubt that this is the last you will see of me," Sopespian said.

Fabian clenched his hand at his side and raised his chin.

"I hope that it is," he said. "Truly, Master Sopespian, I hope that I never see you again."

He turned his head away. The tower's stairwell was a black void, and he descended into its depths.

Journal Entry

Field Notes

A S I APPROACH THE final pages of this journal, it comes to my attention that anyone who finds it may not be entirely clear on the nature of a naiad. And for that, I do not fault them. There has been very little documented over the course of our brief land-bound history. Although there is not much time left to me, I feel it is my responsibility to make note of—at the very least—the most distinguished variations of our species. Bear in mind that I am in no way able to pen, within the bounds of these final pages, a comprehensive guide. Naiads are more varied and numerous than humanity could ever dream to be. And even if one were to search every ocean in the world, and dive into every cavern through the darkest, most crushing depths—there would be more left undiscovered.

That being said, I will specifically focus on six variations, as they bear relevance to the entries and letters that have been recounted here.

Hárkel.

The *Hárkel* are often misconstrued as being of an aggressive variety. My studies have not been able to prove this as a universal truth—rather I have found that those who exhibit abrasive and hostile behaviors, for lack of a better term, are often the exception. They are easily identified by having the most teeth of any other species and are most often found in base shades of dusky blue or grey. Further distinguishing features include their ears, which are the shortest of all and not finned when in full brineskin. Almost all *Hárkel* are known to be poisonous and are subsequently marked by bright, colorful spots, stripes, and freckles to warn of their deadly nature.

Notable. Cahal Ivers. Sopespian Slaine.

Hváll.
The *Hváll* are often referred to, and rightly so, as the songstresses of the sea. In full brineskin, they boast some of the largest members of any pod with the ability to grow up to twenty meters. Their ears are the longest of any type, oftentimes so long that they droop at the tips, and are the most expressive of any naiad (they do wiggle delightfully, I find). Most often grey, although sometimes pale blue, they are known best for their odd singing voices. Not quite like the *Syrena,* as they sing for pleasure and not to hunt. Most *Hváll* are categorized as being even-tempered and gentle.

Notable. Jules Vernon. Ferdinand Bauer.

Áaoll.

The *Áaoll* are best described as slippery and sleek. Of the six varieties, they are the most colorful—I have personally encountered many in base shades of red, blue, yellow, and green. In full brineskin, they have the slimmest tails, which allows them to move quite quickly through even the stormiest waters. I will almost make note that, of any variety, they have the largest fins and the widest eyes, which are often black or milky in color. Because of their slick nature, they have proven the most difficult to capture, much to Her Majesty's disdain.

Notable. Hester Primus. Fabian Wruck.

Höfryngyr.

The *Höfryngyr* are by far the most sociable sort. They travel in the biggest pods and they develop the strongest bonds with one another. Where some naiads tend to separate into smaller groups during one and reconvene during another, *Höfryngyr* travel together year-round and maintain a highly organized social structure. They are considered to be the most intelligent and playful, although of the ones I have met, I cannot speak on that as truth. Most often you will find them in base shades of soft blue, grey, or pink.

Notable. Ephraim Holst.

Örjn.

There is a legend surrounding the *Örjn* that proclaims them to be the 'angels of Tieres'—the ruler of the sea, for those unfamiliar. And while I cannot give you, for certain, whether there is truth in that—I can state, at the very least, that they are rare. The likelihood of encountering one (and surviving, at the very least) is even rarer. They are known to seafarers as winged harpies, and they are the only variety of naiad that spends most of its life above water. Among other differences, they have clawed hands and feet, and of course wings that span over twice their height. I have encountered enough sources that cite the possibility of tails that I will include it in this journal, although I have never observed one and therefore cannot say for certain.

Notable. Aurelius.

Syrena.

The *Syrena* are perhaps the first that spring to mind for many in conversations regarding naiads, although in truth they are hardly naiads at all. They are honorary kin, or perhaps even our ancestors—depending on what source you try to read. They do not travel in pods, although they will gather together to socialize and hunt from time to time before disbanding once again. Where a naiad will consume flesh, the *Syrena* (sirens, to the common seaman) have the most interest in hearts. Even so, when they consume a heart, it is more for sport than for the need of nourishment. They are considered, in many ways, more spirit than properly naiad. They are one of the only varieties that are not limited to oceans and will often travel through saltwater rivers. Most often they are a striking blue, although they can be pink and grey and are often speckled. Their singing voices, unlike the *Höfryngyr*, are utilized for hunting. While a sailor would be quick to fall to its enchantments, it can easily be described as closer to devilish shrieking than an alluring melody.

Notable. Sweeney.

Saltvatnfeld.

A note on the *saltvatnfeld*, or what is known as the brineskin. It is the skin and tail of a naiad when they are in their 'natural state'. When a naiad sheds their brineskin, they will hide it while they walk on land. If someone were to find the skin and take it, that person would then gain control over the naiad until the brineskin was returned. Many naiads in East Avralaen have been enslaved in just this way. In some cases, the brineskin can be destroyed—most notably by burning it. In the case of the skin being destroyed, its holder will lose their control over the naiad, but the naiad will still be unable to return to their natural form and rejoin their home. Having one's brineskin burned is considered to be the most egregious form of torture.

Note. It is worth stating that the *Örjn* and *Syrena* do not possess brineskins. Their natural states are able to exist below and above water.

Note II. Hester Primus was the first to have his brineskin removed. During his capture, Queen Brahntaiste ordered it cut from his body. She claims to have had no knowledge of another way to remove it at the time. After it was cut away, it was burned. It is with this knowledge that I find Hester's acts most condemnable, as he is not completely under the queen's control as he might claim.

The prevailing persecution of naiads in East Avralaen is not to be overlooked. We have always been hunted and harvested for the purposes of mysticism, medicine, and pure vanity. Our bones are turned into charms and sold at markets for good fortune. Our bladders are harvested for perfume, our fat is turned into oil, and our skin is stretched into expensive leather. It is difficult for me to write these truths, such as they are, yet it must be known. There are those who may look upon East Avralaen, and Queen Robin Brahntaiste in particular, as being innovative in finding different uses for us when we are whole. We are her kept prizes, living testimony to East Avralaen's sovereignty and how it extends to even the deepest oceans. It should be seen as nothing more than that. Our lives are no longer ours as soon our feet touch the sand. As soon as we are dragged up in nets and our brineskins are peeled away, the only determining factor of who lives and who is dismembered is pure whim.

We are hated in court, and amongst the Avralaenian people. They belittle us as sexless and undesirable, those who seek out our attentions are considered degenerates of polite society. Those of us who hold positions in court are given bizarre vocations that serve only to other us further. We are astronomers, sorcerers, librarians, and hunters.

We are lords and masters in title only. We are observed, admired, and reviled—never shielded, never cared for. We are as disposable as we are remarkable.

And with that, I will say—it will not continue. We are starting to learn that, in spite of our differences, we have a common enemy to unite against. We must care for one another, keep each other safe, and there will come a time when tyranny will be upended. The Red Tide Monarch will be uncrowned.

End.

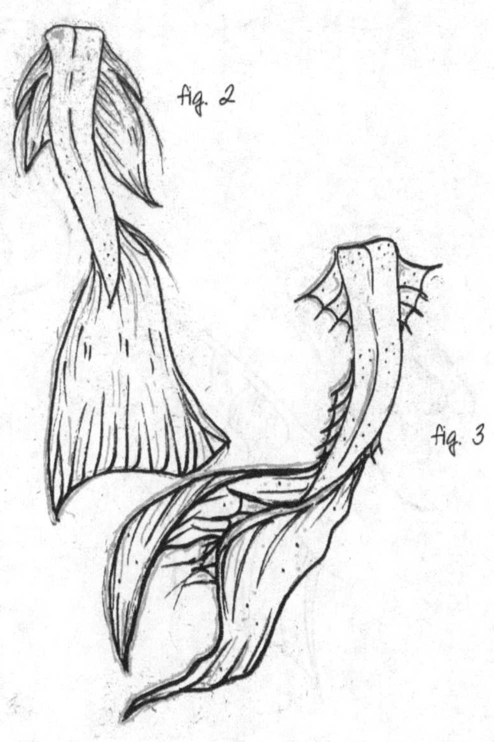

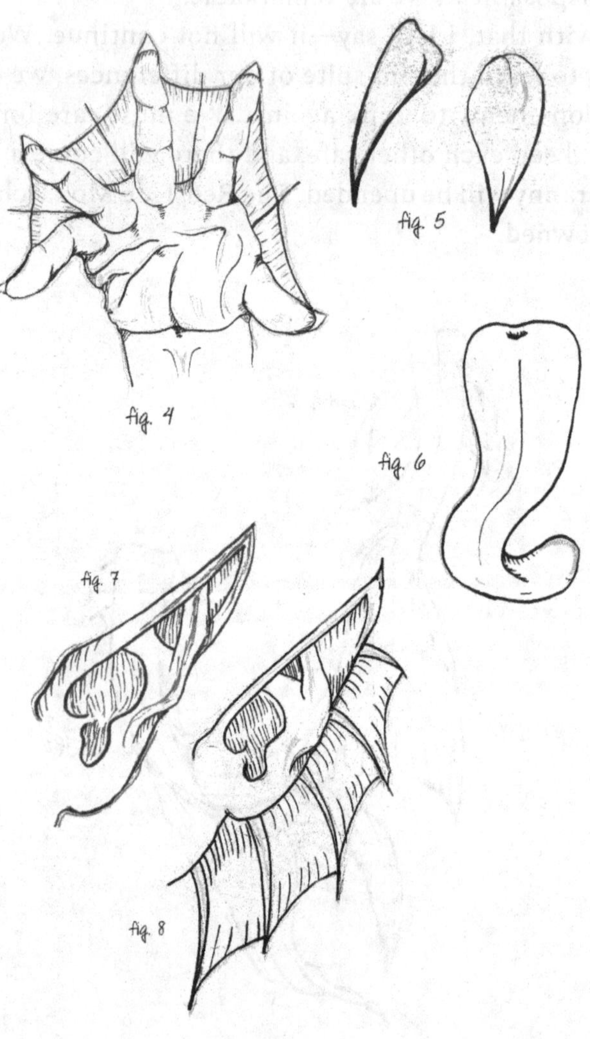

fig. 5
fig. 4
fig. 6
fig. 7
fig. 8

GLOSSARY

AVRALAENIAN.

Borde
sir / used to address someone who is in charge of a group

Mi dhiegh
"my god"

Trebasto
the highest note for a soprano

Múrauch
a derogatory term for naiad meaning 'mud licker'.

Shroudcant
a language comprised entirely of visual gestures and signs

Brebble
the naiad language comprised of clicks, whistles, clacks, and chortles.

V' fontadóire
the chief opera singer of Avralaen's royal court

Strivatta – a form of execution during which the condemned is decapitated with a two-handed saw

DRAGOLOTHIAN.
Den Blauefeall Drinnseet
translates to "The Pale Blue Sea Devil".

Gottsvolden
A greeting, used formally and informally

THE GODS.
Balam
realm of the dead

The Voyager
a masked prophetic sea deity

Tieres
the father god of the sea

ABOUT THE AUTHOR

Sirius is a lover of glory, gore, and monsters. They are a queer, nonbinary artist living in the hot and bothered South; currently residing in a little spot that has been dubbed 'Halloweentown', North Carolina. They are the writer of *The Draonir Saga*, the first book of which is *Uncrowned* (The Laughing Man House), and *The Gentleman Demon Series*, the first book of which is *Swallow you Whole* (Curious Corvid Publishing).

Sirius began writing at a young age and started exploring the publishing industry when they were thirteen. With many bumps along the way, they have learned a lot and grown in the craft that they would consider their one true love. Queer characters, gothic aesthetics, and royal drama (fantasy of manners) form the foundation of their storytelling.

When they are not writing, they work as a professional drag performer, weaving the characters from their stories into visual art for the stage.

You can visit Sirius online at www.uncrownednovel.com.

ACKNOWLEDGMENTS

Ever since I began writing *The Draonir Saga,* the naiads stood out as characters that I wanted a better chance to explore. Their stories are tragic, yes, but humorous and light-hearted as well. They are complex, and I relate to them in many ways. As a group that has been forced to integrate into a society where they do not belong, only to be cast out and shunned by that society, the naiads feel very close to the queer experience. That is what they are, for me, and their stories bring me comfort. I can only hope they might do the same for others.

As far as acknowledgments go, I would like to thank Janus, my editor for this project. Your tireless hours spent combing through every single detail (even the ones that made you go 'ew') really saved me in my eleventh hour. I would like to thank everyone who has really shown their love and support for the world of Draonir. I would be lost without you. To all my readers in the queer community, I love you so very much.

Excerpt from

Hawthorne

A Draonir Novella

Hawthorne

An Excerpt

A thin layer of hard frost laced the corners of the carriage window, encroaching towards the middle with slow but easy confidence and seemingly intent on obscuring Silas' vision. It did not matter much. The sun had long descended behind distant mountain peaks and there were no lamps posted along the winding country road. If there was anything waiting for him out in the darkness, he would not be able to see it until it was too late.

Silas was grateful, at least, for the thick black blanket he had thought to bring with him. His worn coat and gloves were not enough to keep the winter chill from settling down into his bones. Graueyette was a miserable and muddy country by any standard—and its winters were only getting longer and colder. During the peak of the season, the mud would harden and become slicker than ice—and there would be no traveling for months until the gods deigned to look down and extend the mercy of spring.

The carriage jolted as its wheel jammed against a significant dip in the road. Silas braced his hand against the side to keep his head from slamming against it, his other hand moving down to clutch the leather bag nestled snugly against his hip. Despite knowing that it had not left his side since the beginning of his journey, feeling the hard edges of his book through the supple material soothed his anxiety.

He had promised himself that he would not spend too much time picking apart every possible scenario in his head. However, his back ached, and his fingertips were numb. Worrying gave him something else to dwell on.

The patterns of frost on the window were becoming more intricate. Silas bit the inside of his cheek, grinding down on a tab of skin until it disconnected from the flesh with a satisfying pop. It was *Dottore* Sidorov who had extended the invitation and opened the doors of his country manor. He had explicitly referred to himself as an enthusiastic patron of the arts and admitted his eagerness to meet Silas in person with the intent of patronizing his work.

There were so few poets on the continent who ever saw their work as more than troubled scribbles on loose sheets of paper. It had taken Silas over a year to save up enough money to have even one copy transcribed and bound. He had hoped, one day, to be invited to present it in court. Royal patronage was worth its weight in gold, and his name would have been mentioned in the same breath as Claephus, the greatest poet of the age.

A doctor's parlor was not necessarily the audience he had been begging his god for, yet he had snapped up the offer without any hesitation. Sidorov was lauded as a miracle worker and a visionary. He had gold aplenty, and lines of credit that would extend farther than Silas could count. His commendation and his support would mean more printed copies that could be sold, and would, more importantly, be enough to sustain Silas comfortably while he pursued his next great work.

Such things were, of course, completely dependent on the doctor not changing his mind.

The carriage jerked again. Silas closed his eyes, drawing in a deep breath to try and beat back a wave of nausea that threatened to surge up his throat. It had been hours since their last stop and the driver had promised, then, that they were close. Now he had a feeling dawn would arrive at their destination first.

Sleep fought to overtake him. Silas found himself slipping back into its waiting arms, turning around fitful dreams behind his eyelids as he wedged his forehead tightly against a corner to prevent it from knocking with every bump.

He did not hear the carriage door open, but he felt his leg slide. The sudden motion was enough to jolt him back into awareness as he opened his eyes and ground his gloved knuckle into the corners. The driver was already in the process of freeing his singular traveling trunk and setting it down on the gravel. When Silas finally stepped out, the carriage all but heaved to give him up.

Hawthorne releases
October 22nd, 2023